To Morris –
all good wishes !

The March of the 18th

A Story of Crippled Heroes
in the Civil War

BY

Kevin Horgan

PRESS

The March of the 18th
A Story of Crippled Heroes in the Civil War
by Kevin Horgan

Printed in the United States of America

ISBN 9781626971400

This is a work of fiction with a historical basis.

Maps are from the Geography and Map Division, Library of Congress
www.Marchofthe18th.com

www.xulonpress.com

To those who have served,
who are serving now,
and who will someday join the ranks
of the proud citizens defending our nation.

But especially to
those who have given more,
much more than most,
and live with the reality,
what if. . .

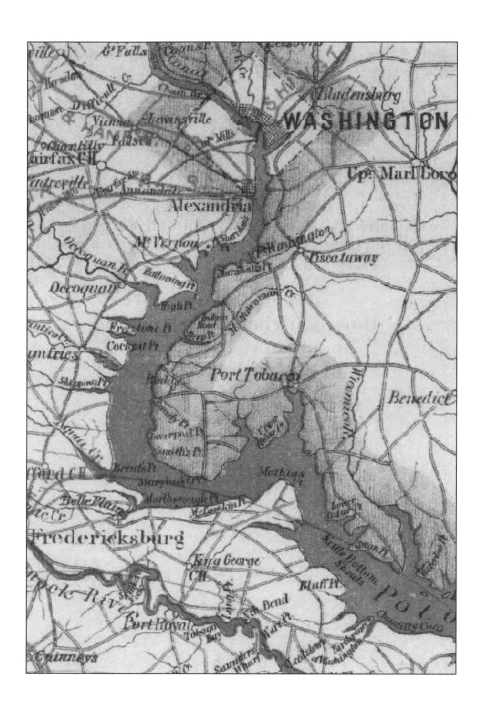

Table of Contents

Part One

For Good

"Do what is good and you will receive approval from it, for it is a servant of God for your good. But if you do evil, be afraid, for it does not bear the sword without purpose; it is the servant of God to inflict wrath on the evildoer."

Romans 13:3-4

1

Today

"Grumpy, can we go to the park after breakfast like we used to?"

A grunt.

"Grumpy? Grumpy?"

"What the heck do you mean, 'Like we used to?' You mean like last week? Yeah, we'll see, Teddy." Burt Scanlon was trying to save his breath, keeping up with his five-year-old grandson. The two, hand in hand, walked steadily up the hill to the strip mall, where they would cross the four lanes to the IHOP at the Four Corners.

"Okay, Grumpy. I'm not tired. Really. But I am hungry. Really."

"Me, neither," Burt struggled to control his breathing, long and deep, and was ready to call a break, as they were only halfway to the IHOP, a full quarter mile to go, mostly uphill.

"Can I rest Grumpy? My foot hurts. But I'm not tired."

"What? Foot? Hurts?" Burt's gasps were compounded by genuine concern.

"My shoe is untied." Teddy pointed down to the Velcro strap of his bright red sneakers.

Relieved, huffing, Burt smiled. "Oh. No problem. Let your Grandpa do that."

Burt was thankful for the rest. He and Teddy had been to the IHOP early on Saturday many times by car, but the cool spring morning was too much to resist. This was their first time hoofing it.

I'm in no hurry now, Burt thought, take your time; I'm not that old, but I'm not that young, either. He made a show of examining the shoe, fastening the strap, then listened intently to Teddy's elbow, which brought the predictable giggles.

"You're silly, Grumpy. Can we go? I'm a hungry boy."

"It'll be there when we get there, you little peckerhead." Burt half-smiled, winked at Teddy, and they began walking again, slower. Teddy swung his arm, holding Burt's hand tightly.

Saturday morning traffic is even less than church traffic around here, Burt mused, folks driving here and there. Why did I think I could walk this?

The boys stood at the Four Corners' traffic light, across the street from the big blue roof. The lights were interminably long, the left turns inhibiting easy crossing. They could have walked straight across with the light traffic, but the boy was five and every safety precaution was needed. Set an example, Granddad. Maybe stop calling him peckerhead, too.

They got to the crossing too late, so the three minute wait, even this early on a Saturday, commenced. Burt looked down at his grandson, who was beaming back up at him.

He's a wonder, thought Burt. He smiled back in amazement. I don't recall looking at my grandfather like that.

They both looked back across the street, watching the nearest car in the restaurant parking lot stop and then reverse back into an open space.

"Smooth job," said Burt.

"Smart to back in, right Grumpy?"

"Yes, Teddy bear, always leave yourself an out."

The driver opened his door, and his left leg arced out. From the knee down it was a metal prosthetic with a sneaker at the end. The driver emerged standing quickly, if initially unsteadily, and met the boys' eyes. He nodded, grinned mildly, and walked erect, glancing down more than up toward the IHOP entrance.

A horn honked.

"Can we cross, Grumpy?"

"Yes, yes, let's do it, Teddy." They quick-stepped through the intersection, and bounced together, happily, into the restaurant.

"Hello, Major!" The waitress half cooed, half bellowed on seeing Burt, "And your cute friend, too!"

"Good morning, Ladasha, your finest table, please!"

The place had not really cranked up yet, but the lot was starting to bulge and the customers steadily trickled in. Ladasha led the boys to a window booth, across from the counter, away from the door.

"I'll bring you handsome fellas some coffee and cocoa in just a sec."

Ladasha was lyrical and happy, a mainstay of the restaurant, and she loved her regular customers as if they were family she knew wouldn't stay long. Good to see you, enjoy yourself, too bad you have to leave, we'll do this again real soon.

The drinks came, and Burt asked for water. He was sweating more than he planned. He sipped his coffee, Teddy sipped his cocoa. When Ladasha brought the water (how does that big girl move so fast?), Burt had an impulse.

"Who's the guy with the leg at the counter?"

"Oh, he's a soldier, been visiting his sister here, she lives off the park. Poor thing lost his leg over there a year or so ago. He's so handsome. I'm just gonna bite him."

Teddy laughed conspiratorially, and Burt said, "Let me get his check. Please."

"Oh, I just may take a bite out of both you! Now what'll you men have today?"

"Ham and eggs, over easy, rye toast. How about you, Peck--, uh, Teddy bear?"

"Strawberry pancakes, please!"

"Coming right up, guys," and she whisked herself away.

Their meal was served, and Teddy reflexively folded his hands and closed his eyes, moving his lips in imitation of others. Burt stared at him. He is a wonder, my grandson.

The boys were chewing and slurping, content in silence, as Ladasha brought over two small glasses of milk.

"My soldier friend sent these over for you," smiling and moving away.

Both with mouthfuls, Burt raised his glass and turned to the soldier at the counter, who raised his coffee, smiled, and nodded. Teddy waved.

"Can we drink the milk, Grumpy?"

"Sure, Teddy. It's a gift. I covered his breakfast; it's a very nice thank you, kind of a joke, really. Oh. . ."

Burt lurched, lifted his hip, instant realizing, then visualizing, his wallet on the kitchen table at home.

"Oh, *nuts.*"

"Hi!" Teddy beamed, and the one-legged soldier was at their table, smiling at Teddy, looking sideways at Burt.

"Oh, hey," Burt half stood, extending his hand. "Burt Scanlon, this is Teddy."

"Good morning. Clarence Finney. Thank you for breakfast, sir."

"And thank you for the milk. Grumpy never gets milk or juice 'cause it's too much money. He says we can come more often if we don't spend too much, right Grumpy?"

Burt groaned.

"You okay, sir?"

"Just Burt, please. Have a seat, won't you, Clarence, right?"

"Yes. Sure, thanks." He slid in next to Teddy.

The boy stared open-mouthed, first to the soldier's leg, then slowly up to his face, then back to his leg.

Clarence smiled warmly, "So, Teddy, uh, is it the leg or you haven't seen a black man this close?"

Teddy's eyes grew wider. Burt laughed, "Maybe a little of both. You were army, in the Gulf?"

"Yeah, both Iraq and Afghanistan. Made the Iraq tour without a headache, came home, and two years later was only in country in Afghanistan for three weeks when our supply convoy hit an IED. I don't want to remember much; spent too much time in hospitals. But I was lucky."

The silence was broken by the innocence of the question.

"Does it hurt, Mr. Clarence?"

"No. Well, sometimes. You get used to it. But I do have what I need, little friend. Maybe the Lord walks with me."

"I'm sure He does," Burt said thickly. "Thanks for your service, Clarence. I was in the marines, post-Vietnam. Never shot at, thank God."

Clarence was suddenly expansive. "Marines, huh? You look like you were a bad wagon back in your day. Were they still using sails on ships in the department of the Navy to get you jarheads around?" Smiling, baiting like all servicemen reflexively do.

"The men's department, son." Right back at him, on cue.

"Is Clarence a peckerhead, too, Grumpy?"

Clarence let his head rock back, slapped his hand on the table, and roared in laughter, scaring the whole restaurant.

Burt reddened deeply. Teddy smiled.

"Grumpy says I'm a peckerhead when he gets that face, Mr. Clarence, so I think you might be a peckerhead, too."

Clarence whooped again, louder if that was possible, and tears streamed down one side of his face, he was laughing so hard.

Burt was nearly crying from embarrassment.

"Can I touch your skin?"

Clarence steadied his breath, heaved a small sigh, and smiled softly, "Sure, Teddy." And Teddy put his fingertips on Clarence's arm and let his fingers glide from elbow to wrist.

"Grumpy's arm is real hairy. So is my dad's. You don't have much."

"Well, Grumpy. . ." But Clarence couldn't finish the sentence, and started laughing again. Ladasha arrived with the check. Burt shot out of the booth, turning her away.

"I forgot my wallet, Ladasha, I feel terrible. I'll go home and get it and drive right back."

Ladasha feigned indignation. "Hmmph! That's okay, major. I know where you live."

"I'll be back soon, sorry, oh God I feel terrible."

Her eyes smiled. "Shush, now."

"Grumpy, can Clarence come to the park with us? Clarence you can drive and we'll walk. Can you come, please? Please?"

"Maybe, little friend."

"Now, Teddy, Clarence may have plans."

"Pleeeeeeease."

Burt grimaced and glanced to where Clarence's prosthetic would be if he could see through the table.

"My leg is fine, Burt. I know what you're thinking."

"Oh, uh, no, but. . ."

Clarence smiled and sighed. "I would have stayed a soldier, if they would have let me. I liked the life. I like the people. I had talked about doing my twenty, you know, had a real plan." Clarence looked out the window. "But this is where I am now. Sure, Teddy, I can walk to the park. I can do anything, my friend."

Burt knew the day had promise. It was going to be a beauty, he thought, and he noticed little things in the walk to the park, the morning mist now fully lifted, traffic starting to jump, a great day. . .

2

Yesterday, 1863

★

. . . *a* nd a great war seized a nation that wrested with good and evil. Each army had wrought unforeseen damage and destruction on both man and property, and there was no end in sight. Each army believed it fighting and dying and shedding blood for the good. Large conflicts became part of history, lore and legend, but a thousand stories with thousands unnamed in battles unrecorded happened too often to memorialize. In all, the uniform of either army was for the good, the victor measured by who walked away. In all, a thread of evil did not wear either blue or grey.

The dew-like fog hung in the leaves and fell downward, kissing the needles and branches and rock under their feet. There was no road here. The soldier followed the soldier in front of him, not knowing where he was headed but praying the march would end with rest and without a shot fired. The soldier did not know that the two columns on the march through the light thicket were being led by an untested officer who knew the terrain and was avoiding any roads to get to the company's appointed departure line, in order to engage the enemy before dark. The midday attack plan may have been ill-conceived, but twilight combat was suicidal.

The young lieutenant was certain that his platoon of over thirty soldiers could traverse the woods, quietly set up a skirmish line, and march headlong into an outlier of the Fredericksburg perimeter, using the woods as cover until the rebels were in musket range. The lighter the day the better, he thought, I don't want to engage in the dark. Hence the short-cut.

The lieutenant did not know that a larger company, led by a major commissioned as a political favor, was taking the road the lieutenant could have used. The major, hard-featured and soft-willed, had been manipulated by his first sergeant who could fight but not think tactically. All the men have sore feet, the sergeant complained, so the beaten path would save us for battle. The major leapt at the chance to be liked, for a false reason, at the wrong time. The major's unit was to be a rear guard, held in reserve of the lieutenant's late day fast strike assault and retrograde. His company was to defend against penetration from the east, and provide a defense and safe haven for the planned retreat of the platoon.

The major was a poor land navigator, relying on his unde-veloped instinct and a boy private who professed knowledge of the area, "in my youth," which was explosively funny except no one saw it that way. The major, his first sergeant, and all the men in the command trusted the private because they wanted to believe the soft shaded road was their path to an easy defensive night.

There would be no artillery in support of the lieutenant's attack. The mission was to create havoc, determine the perim-eter defensive positions of the enemy, and retreat in an orderly fashion east northeast and fall in behind the defensive line of the major's company. That rear guard would have numerous pickets in place, anticipating an orderly, fast retreat, blue coats on the double time to friendly lines. The men joked that as long as there was no rebel yell, they wouldn't shoot.

The platoon made good time, but the brightness of the day hindered swift movement as it neared the objective. The lieu-tenant halted the platoon, and prayed the major would have his defensive line in place. The young officer's folly of a quick march was evident as the sun shone directly above the tree line he would need for his platoon's cover. The opportunity for concealment would have no value until the sun ducked under the tree line, which forced him to estimate a wait, an hour, maybe more. The risk of discovery was growing greater by the minute. If a stray dog runs into these trees, he knew, we are found and we are dead.

The lieutenant passed the word for silence, for ready on my command, for patience, waiting for the sun to dip down just a little more, then we'll move. Garbled, contrary and complicated orders are often mocked and truncated, and halfway down the line the message was "be quiet, but ready." The NCOs placed the company several yards into the tree line, deep in the shade.

The sun was directly in their eyes. They waited.

Just north and east, the major's company took the meandering path to a fork. The left was rough and possibly private. The right was smooth and wide enough for four horses abreast.

The major looked at the private who bragged of his knowledge, from his youth.

"Is this familiar to you?"

The private stared, slack mouthed, and looked directly above him to a clear sky. He knew the objective was due west, that this fork was probably far enough for the major's intent. He heard the sounds of civilization echo and was about to speak.

"This corner may be an excellent placement for the company, sir," the first sergeant said. "We can send out pickets on the sides of both roads, deep, and the lieutenant's platoon may use either one back to us."

The major was unconvinced. Although the march was three hours, it did not seem they went far enough. He had relied on the private and the first sergeant and had not assigned a pace count. The day was cool and shaded and uneventful. The thought of having a defensive posture, and a boy lieutenant earning the glory of the engagement, had been pressing into his mind for miles.

The location was ideal.

"Let's move closer. They may need stronger support."

"Which path?"

"The narrow one. We'll be concealed."

@@@

The rebel soldier was on alert with the rest of his platoon, but the midday coolness of shade had him and each man more relaxed than anxious. The breeze moved west to east, rolling through the trees, whistling low and faint and masking any sounds coming into the pasture. Some of the platoon slept. Some stared impassively from the breastworks, a loosely reinforced defensive construction chest-high. They had been without an officer or leadership or heavy weapons for a week now. The rebel soldier thought they might have been forgotten, and a good thing, too.

He had to use the privy. He stood, stretched, and left his weapon at his defensive firing position. It was a good spot, and that rat from Charleston wanted it, and he'd give him hell to pay if he took it.

"Watch my spot. Back in a few minutes." He took off quickly, using a gait that minimized sound and disruption, though no one had really cared in days. The platoon was alone, and would likely stay that way. Many civilians moved in and out and through the little outpost. The slit trench latrine the command required was far back from the tree line and false corn crib that masked the breastworks, providing just enough darkness for modesty. Soldiers always take the easy opportunity to relieve themselves, but now the near location stank horrifically, so he dove deeper into the wood, toward the end of the trench. The rebel hustled quicker now as the need to go became urgent.

He never saw the two large figures in long coats rigid near the end of the latrine. He found a spot, untied his trousers, and squatted holding a low branch, and was struck on the side of his head by what he thought, for an instant, might be a large bee. The soldier turned on his heels, nearly fell in the trench, and the last image he registered was two imposing men, one with a flaming red beard, and the other with a single snarl of a tooth grinning at him.

The man with the red beard hit him left, then right with his fists, the second punch short and powerful under the jaw that snapped the soldier's head back, and in a slow arc he fell backward, impaling his head on an odd sharp stone with a wet thunk. The rebel never breathed a sound. His bowels released.

"Oh, damn all, Red, you killed him," whined the one-tooth man.

Redbeard grinned broadly, gnarly greenish-grey teeth speckled under the color of the beard. "Hah! Couldn't have done that to his head if I wanted to, Dogtooth. Hah," he whispered hoarsely.

"But he's dead with grease all over."

"Quiet. You don't get to bugger him, so what. I got what I wanted, Dog."

"Why you'll be damned forever, Red. Damned forever."

"Shut up, you idiot. We need money and food and weapons and whatever we can sell or barter. I kill any man for what I need. This rebel kills men because someone tells him to, to protect keeping Negras as property. He's almost as pathetic as the union boys, who would die to free the Negras." Redbeard got close to Dogtooth. "I laugh at them. They think they're heroes. But they are better than you, Dog. You is a pederast."

"You told me that was okay."

"It's okay when I can threaten someone with the likes of your, uh, appetite. That last boy told us every thing hidden in that barn, didn't he? Hah! And you had him anyway, hah!"

Dogtooth looked at the dead soldier.

Redbeard spoke low, "I take my pleasure in the torture of others, Dog, that's why I keep you around. Check his pockets, see if he's got anything worthwhile. . ."

The first volley from the pasture rang out.

"Flee."

The two men ran pell mell through the woods, heedless of the sound made as the cacophony of weapon fire covered any noise they could muster.

The rebel soldier, dead, stared blankly upwards. If he could, he would have seen leaves rustling, green and black and grey, and through them even higher the sky so blue his eyes would have ached. Had the marauders checked the young man's pockets, they would have found no food or money. There was only one letter, grimy and sweat streaked, from a young girl professing love and to please please come home to her.

@@@

The lieutenant believed the sun stopped moving at all.

A husky sergeant moved gracefully, swiftly, to the lieutenant's position.

"Sir," he whispered. "I swear there's a large troop movement behind us, may be a quarter mile, moving quick and loud."

The lieutenant was torn, confused. The rear guard line was to be much further away, on the main road, not in the woods. Could this be an enemy envelopment? His eyes were unfocused, the sun having bleached his judgment.

The sun fell, and touched the top of the tree line.

"We can't attack two fronts. Sergeant, keep a squad about twenty five yards back, in case it's the major. We're gonna attack now."

"Hup."

Clinks of metal, then silence, the high pitched screed of silence, constant, unyielding, piercing through and enveloping nature's peace. Rebel soldiers seemingly froze in the distance ahead, the major's movement coming hard behind, still unidentified and unready for battle.

"Charge!"

Twenty three men on a line charged headlong into the field, the rebels scrambled but still unseen, and then the breastworks hard left opened fire on the running soldiers. The blast came first from six rifles, then a volley of ten. At the start no one fell, then five, then five more; then all pitched face first to the ground, a washboard pasture for sheep and goats. The sounds of rebels reloading told the lieutenant all he needed to know. He was outflanked, if not outgunned, and the main origin of defensive fire came from what appeared to be a corncrib, but what was actually a well-reinforced and established battlement.

The lieutenant was in the middle of the line, and the first squad on the extreme left caught the brunt of it. Attack or retreat? He paused. The remaining platoon waited an eternity in the seconds it took to catch its collective breath, and the rebels to reload.

@@@

"Major?" From the husky sergeant, standing with arms spread.

The major rushed to him. "Yes, has the attack started?"

"More like an ambush, sir. The platoon is pinned down in the pasture there."

The major's first sergeant took over. "To the tree line, I see where the fire is from."

The major's company was quickly moved into position, hard left, a first line prone, then one kneeling, then one standing. The volleys of fire into the pasture masked the sounds of men and orders and checking weapons, smooth by necessity, and inevitably lethal.

Silence again. The rebels behind the breastworks surveyed the pasture and several popped up to obtain a better look. The muskets and guns of the major's company had the range, and a clear field of fire.

"On your command, sir."

"Fire at will."

The first volley from the standing line was tremendous, the corncrib breastworks coughing wood, dirt, stone, and blood.

@@@

"Wheel left, open fire," shouted the lieutenant and his remaining platoon stood and turned, instinctively knowing that they had support now but also needing to take fate into their own hands. Weapons ready, their first volley was very accurate, closer to the objective.

"Every shot, move closer two paces."

This particular drill was fraught with problems, but the soldiers followed confidently expressed orders even when logic told them to fall and cover themselves.

The rebel fire withered, and then there was a rush of stampeding feet away from the breastworks.

The left wheel maneuver worked well, surprising everyone in its audacity, especially the rebels in the corncrib turned battlement. The lieutenant, within twenty yards of the breastworks, now fully on line, shouted charge; the major in the tree line commanded cease fire, and the rebels did not fire another shot that day.

Both sides demonstrated bravery and both fought with skill, though today ineptitude was rewarded by random good fortune, for the blue. Several rebels died anonymously and were left in place. The union forces did not pursue those who retreated, but moved back the way they came, according to their mission plan.

To a man, none would see Christmas that year.

And only evil survived.

@@@

3

Kuriger and Time

*A*merica was becoming mournful with fatigue and death. The values of a large swath of Virginia, North Carolina, Tennessee, Mississippi and Louisiana had embraced the lowest nature of man, that anything was fair game for marauders, that death was a just way to deal with theft, that non-capitulation to irrational orders real and perceived could be dealt with conclusively, finally and brutally quick. Verdant scenery turned grey with the blood of innocence lost, and uniforms of both armies became charcoal with filth. The dirt infected the soul. Men moved forward because staying in place was giving in to dying.

The cool clear air from above gently settled on the tree tops and folded then cascaded through leaves and pushed branches aside to rush to the virgin forest floor below. From the ground, the heat rose sharply, oppressively, thick with the afternoon's humidity, swirling in light and shade. The shade yielded. The heat prevailed. Trees drew all moisture to themselves from deep within the lush earth.

Marching soldiers touched leaves, plucked the greenest, then bit and sucked greedily at the false promise of moisture. The narrow trail coaxed the column into alignment, barely two abreast, as men tried to avoid the unavoidable, the relentless sun. Step after step, pulled down to the cooler earth in the narrow folds of fingers and draws before an officer or a purposeful soldier reminds them that every step downhill will require two steps up. All are too weak to quarrel. All are too weary to comply with the inexorable logic that they cannot rest until they are told to stop. So they keep moving, step after step.

Step after step. Lift, scrape, heel to toe; wincing, lift, scrape, toe, heel; wincing, lift, scrape, flat sole strike and fall like a stone. Soles, heels, toes raw and piercing, insteps hotter than the air. Step after step; lift and scrape and wince.

Eyes front, a safe march. Look below at the cool earth, so far away, inviting rest. Look above at the blue white sky through the green grey leaves. Hot, humid, and thick where they breathe. Step after step.

@@@

Abram Kuriger was old and ageless when the war began, then in his late thirties. Lanky, sinewy, dark featured with bulging eyes, his voice a force in itself, a commanding cadence that mocked the echo of cannons even in the heat of it, a gravelly yet clear dictation of orders when in garrison. Single barked commands were preceded by nothing but a short cough, whether one word "halt" or a litany of profanity on a poorly attended latrine, or ceaseless orders in battle for correction, for encouragement, for fear, for moving directly into the fire of the rebels.

Sergeant Kuriger's eyes never strayed from his direct front. He moved his head from one side, then the other, or up, or down. Kuriger's eyes never shifted from where his nose was directed. His voice never cracked from strain or fatigue. He was a model soldier, born for the duty of leading men in a fight, preparing men to follow orders, to kill without hesitation.

Kuriger had killed many. In order to lead men, to direct the fight, to keep others in line, and to secure objectives, Kuriger used his weapon infrequently. An army may be inspired by generals, but sergeants executed. When Kuriger killed, it was with his hands or his knife. His large-boned arms, like knotted oak, were dangerously strong, and his fist, gnarled, split and roughened, could strike a man dead in one blow. And had.

The old sergeant had fought Indians, but was no skilled horseman. He suffered silently through the boredom of garrison life in small posts in the Plains, where dirt was everywhere and in everything, and water and horses were the essence of the army's life.

Such tedium had consequences. Years before, in the north Texas territory on a thick hot night he had too much whiskey after too much work and too little food and rest, and had killed a gambler in a fight over a lamb shank, even though the meat was maggot-ridden, supper for the floor sweeper and spittoon cleaner. Kuriger remembered little, except that Providence shone on him that night. The man he beat to death, even more inebriated, was a poor gambler but a skilled horse thief, and was to hang anyway when the law caught up. Kuriger, then a corporal, was hailed a hero by local civilians, and all witnesses were breathless at the devastation of his hammer of a right hand. Though the army knew better, that Kuriger was drunk and acted in a misguided stupor, the commanding officer saw an exploitable asset.

Men fear dangerous men. Men admire those who protect lesser brothers who sweep and clean. Civilians who surround and support a military garrison need to believe their sacrifices for the soldiers they harbor are not in vain. That heroes do live in time of relative peace. The inquiry and swift dismissal of the assault and one-punch death was conducted in a horse stall, the sheriff beaming that justice was served and relieved that he did not have to risk serving it.

Captain Jon Time promoted Kuriger to sergeant that day.

Thrust into authority, the senior enlisted man of a platoon of regulars, Kuriger aged quickly, without distinction; without problem, too, for several in the platoon witnessed his close combat power. Now a favorite of the company's commander,

Kuriger was taught, obliquely through the routine machinations of garrison life, that a commanding voice and an intense visage would compel men to do anything, especially if not inclined to do so. The threat of his fist, now mythical, was enough to keep his platoon disciplined.

The army had improved Abram Kuriger's life. He returned the good grace by saving the men in its infantry and cavalry, each day. The war in turn would save Kuriger's life.

@@@

By the time the war was midway through its first year, Kuriger was constantly training or watching men being killed, encouraging his soldiers to maintain their heads, and finding opportunity for ground gain in the absence of direction. He cared for his soldiers; their fear of both death and their sergeant compelled them, individually and collectively, to be model soldiers relied upon by Kuriger and their officers for mission execution.

By the time the war had entered the third year, Kuriger was more intent on the survival of those in his charge, and cynically supported the idea that the security of Washington, D.C., was paramount. He vowed to provide what leadership he could at all times.

Early skirmishes and the horror of Bull Run focused the efforts of McClellan's army around the repetition of drill, drill, drill. A massed force is only as strong as its weakest link, some said, and the individual soldier's ability to execute commands under duress was the great unknown of battle. The early clashes of the war made for tall stories, sometime heroics, and opportunities for ambitious leaders. That the opportunity came as a result of high officer casualty rates was immaterial. Wars are fought by soldiers, and soldiers must be led.

@@@

In the spring of the war's third year, Jon Time, at 40 years and now a colonel, was leading a regiment, the only surviving officer of his unit, save one, from Bull Run two years before. Time, broad shouldered of medium height, did not look like the dashing figure of McClellan, but his carriage was imperial. Time was ruthless in battle, unconcerned about his personal safety. He was not a merciful man. Pragmatic by nature, he saw his own mortality as secondary to the greater cause, and it showed from his set of jaw. Time's reputation was well-established, a true leader in war, and the respect from his men, that so often eludes the most professional of officers, was genuine and heartfelt.

Time's great concern was his subordinate leadership, the lack of experience, and the taming of the impetuous. Better to temper the hot head, he believed, than try to breathe fire into a slow-witted officer. He blessed his own good fortune in having First Sergeant Kuriger available to shape the leadership of the young in his command.

Time was indulgent toward those soldiers who were strong and independent, and he cultivated their skills passionately. He also tended toward too much empathy for the very young soldier, seeing only a child's fear, yet he brooked no cowardice from those he deemed capable, and Time's judgment was as final as it was arbitrary. Only another cold and hardened warrior could discern the difference, and all others be damned.

4

Four Mile

*W*ill Anderson was raised in some comfort, though his family believed strongly in the rigors of an outdoor life. He learned to hunt using trap, bow, and gun, with a skill nurtured by his proud father, but was weak in execution. Their bond tightened year after year as four sisters followed, and he and his father, Tom Anderson, became inseparable.

Tom, a stern man of modest but steady means, saw his son as delicate of both frame and mind. By setting a hearty rugged standard for young Will to grow into manhood, Tom hoped to avoid what he believed to be young Will's mild tendencies. While he may have been disappointed by young Will's execution of outdoor skills, he could not deny that his son gave it everything he had, even if that was woefully short. The boy just favored his mother's size and temperament.

"The effort, lad, will bear fruit. Never give up on the task at hand. Never let go."

@@@

Tom Anderson had been a plebe at West Point, more than two decades before, but had barely completed a year before he was required home. A typhoid outbreak had lay waste and death to nearly half the town of Four Mile, including his parents and two brothers. The hamlet was called Four Mile because it was four miles west of Mingo Junction, Ohio, not a bustling town but with a foundry.

Tom returned to a small grocery and home sustaining farm, with no desire or skill to keep them solvent. He left his ambition of West Point behind him, at first to mourn. As the enormity and finality of the disease's swath through Four Mile became all too clear, he was bound to stay to rebuild the town. At 17 years of age, with only a few months of West Point education to draw upon, he was seen by the surviving townsfolk not as a bewildered youth overwhelmed with grief, but as the raw clay of an untested but willing leader.

Tom worked and organized and cajoled tirelessly. It was less about survival than about ensuring everyone in Four Mile had a vital task to contribute. Not returning to West Point enraged him in quieter moments, and in order to bury that anger Tom went without rest, ensuring a fresh water supply was established, burning infected clothes and bedding, equally distributing foodstuff and blankets and tools and animals, and accidently anointing a new pastor. Families were overwhelmed with the burial of the dead, and the routine comforts of modern life on the edge of the frontier of 1837 were beyond the limits of most folks' comprehension. Barbers became tanners, fence builders became sanitary engineers and well-diggers, horse doctors became midwives, midwives became doctors. If you could read, and see the consequence of one action far ahead of the immediate, you were in charge. And Tom Anderson could read.

Artisans and the soft had survived while the rugged settlers had passed away. Within a week of returning, Tom could see the heaviness of abject defeat on the faces of everyone. The widow of an ironsmith started organizing a small exodus of townspeople on a one horse wagon and a couple sleds, most of the people with only rags on their backs, with no food. Her authority came from her girth and that she alone was able to shoe and bridle a horse efficiently. Hands on hips, hair wild, apron filthy with grease and dirt, Mrs. MacClenny cut an imposing figure. She'll send them all to oblivion, Tom thought, I need to stop this. We cannot run.

"Where will you go?" he exclaimed. "Word has spread. They think we're a dead town. That we carry disease. We need to show we can stand here, and make our town survive this. We cannot run from our heritage. We cannot run from the graves of our loved ones. We owe them that honor." Tom shook from head to foot. He had heard that speech in eerily similar forms every day for over six months, echoes off the Hudson. The cry of desperate students, soon to be soldiers, thrust into leadership, to the last.

"But God left us. We need to follow Him."

This from a wisp of a girl, thin, slight, hips awkwardly flared, a fawn about to grow strong. And wild brown hair.

"Shush, Brigit, I tell you God is always with us, even now," said Mrs. MacClenny to her only surviving child, not yet twelve.

A crowd pressed in. It was hard to speak of God, as the preacher and his wife and all their four children passed in one dreadful night. The church, on the crest above the pines, built only last year, was the jewel of the town, and no one wanted to sully the sanctuary with their cursed disease.

"Mama, we should go pray, please, for God to come back, or to show Himself." Brigit's eyes were hollow, deep black from hunger, exhaustion and fear. The crowd murmured assent. Mrs. MacClenny raised her hands slowly to her head, on the edge of a scream, then looked heavenward and thrust her arms outstretched to the sky.

"Yes, yes, we need to pray! Yes, we need to beseech God now!"

The herd moved first woodenly, leaving belongings in the dirt road. The mass then walked expectantly, and by the time Mrs. MacClenny and Brigit had walked hand in hand the hundred yards or so to the church door, the remnants of odd town survivors were running to catch up.

Inside the church, after a time, shoulder to shoulder, the ladies and children were seated, with the men standing along the walls or kneeling in the center aisles. Mrs. MacClenny and Brigit sat in the front pew. They were Catholic, of sorts; this was not their church. Tom strode with trepidation to the lectern.

"Dear Lord. We need a sign you are with us. We need your strength and forgiveness. We humbly ask for your love and pity." He stopped, and looked out. Barely half the ramshackle congregation could look at him. Brigit beamed. Mrs. MacClenny, crying, moved a wild strand of Brigit's hair from her child's eyes.

Tom couldn't carry it. He could only delay desertion. He had borne much these past few weeks, but not from wisdom. The town was beaten. It needed more.

"Mrs. MacClenny, would you lead us in song?" Tom's voice had the timber to snap the crowd's lethargy. Mrs. MacClenny jumped as if stabbed with a needle, and she strode to the lectern, and began to sing. Everyone followed. The windows shook from the roar of their voices raised in song.

Four Mile had a preacher. A Catholic widow who could shoe a nag and raise a sweet girl amidst the pallor and stench of death saved them with song. Four Mile would survive.

@@@

Tom married Brigit three years later. Brigit had blossomed in those years, and Four Mile grew and kept its people. The trails became roads and the homes became shops and the children became parents, and the town grew stronger and sturdier and pilgrims came to it, one family at a time.

Brigit's first two children were stillborn. The Ohio winters were harsh, their home drafty and damp. Tom redoubled his effort in maintaining his business, and neighbors knew they owed him much for his sacrifice. Brigit provided sunshine for the whole town, but she couldn't hold a child beyond her womb. The young couple's desperation was absorbed by those closest, and their home took on a warmer, more secure cradle for their help. Tom kept goods flowing into town, and brought physical and financial security through his innate organizational skills. Brigit had learned to read and write early at her mother's knee and taught every child in Four Mile who could spare the time.

Another year passed. Mrs. MacClenny reluctantly acquiesced to the town's general opinion and conceded the informal parson mantle to a real preacher, newly arrived, who feared God but loved children and was grateful for his flock.

Tom had become a man of energy, ideas, and the backbone to see them through. He could also talk until the fire burned out, and most everyone listened, politely and respectfully, even though they had heard the stories enough to finish Tom's thoughts.

Many of Tom Anderson's yarns were of his brief time at West Point. He told a decade's worth of fable and fact for his six month's attendance. Tom would summon the cadence of the parade ground while describing the rustle of autumn leaves striking the impenetrable stone of the main buildings, the full moon on the Hudson, the smell of sweat as the cadets retired for the night, the promise of another run at honor in the moments before reveille on a fog-shrouded winter's morning.

And of friendships. Tom spoke highly of a young cadet one year ahead of him, who embodied the soldier he wanted to be. William Tecumseh Sherman was no parade deck martinet, Tom always stressed, but a quick witted sharp eyed young man dedicated to the profession, not the trappings. Sherman exuded a confidence beyond his years, and his peers and other underclassmen were drawn to his serious nature.

The passage of time and distance takes the pettiness out of a soldier's memory, and past casual glances can be manifested as martial and heroic encounters. Sometimes, too, with acquaintances, especially when the friendship is not equally returned. Tom always believed that William Tecumseh Sherman was watching his own struggle that fall and into the winter of 1837, as often as he daydreamed of receiving his own commission, an achievement that was never to be.

In 1843, Four Mile was annexed to Mingo Junction, the larger town nearby, though the original settlers would always refer to Four Mile. Legitimacy was more important than water that spring, and Tom pushed hard to join with the next municipality. His reward was an appointed captaincy in the Mingo Junction's budding militia. Tom embraced the honorarium, and vowed to live up to his largely paper rank.

Six years after the plague, as the people of Mingo Junction called it, the first parade was held, complete with singing and music and marching men, followed by happy women, children, and barking dogs. It was brief, as good ceremonies should always be, an organized walk from MacClenny's now expanded stable to the church by the pines, and then back to the stables, and laughably back to the church since the new parson insisted it should end there.

That day William Tecumseh Anderson was baptized, as bright and glorious a day as ever remembered.

@@@

Young Will's birth was hailed, and the Andersons' good fortune was made better, as four sisters followed in rapid succession. Young Will was constantly at his father's side, when practical. Although he was enthused about being the man he believed his father expected him to be, his slight frame and gentle nature eclipsed any progress, physically, and his confidence suffered from a tender age as his sisters outran and outworked him.

Tom Anderson, known through the next two decades as the Captain, could see his son struggle. Not for a lack of effort, he thought; he is a good son and shall always be able to look after his mother when I am gone.

Will watched the Captain with an intensity bordering on rapture, and was especially focused on militia drills. The Captain elevated Will's status in the town by keeping him in formation at all times, and encouraging the youngster to drill with the volunteers. He was tolerated, if not completely accepted. Will's ineptness with basic military skills was acknowledged.

Will could always sense the disappointment from others, but his father constantly exhorted his young son to never give up.

"Father, why do you lead the militia? Why spend so much time with me at your side?"

"Because you are watching."

@@@

August 1863

Father, your letters give me purpose, and strength. I will always struggle with courage, and I still shake before I speak to men in my charge. I do not wish to shame the honor of our uniform, and as an officer I am relied on to do more than set the example but that is all I can try to summon now. I think I have acquitted myself honorably if without effect and certainly absent any courage in all our engagements. The Lord has seen to give me strong NCOs who are battle savvy and cool of temperament. They have guided me in making decisions. I have been wise in taking their solicitous advice.

Sergeants run this soldier's army. I believe that if sergeants were commanding, this war would end swiftly.

I surprised myself in the fight. I disappointed myself as I went to the sound not for the objective, or even to kill the enemy. I charged to live. I cannot husband that necessary zeal for closing with and engaging the enemy. I still do not know if I can be brave enough to sacrifice my fear, give into my fright and act if the situation calls for me to do so. I think of you, father, that I will honor your name, our name, when the time comes.

Your obedient son, Lt W. Tecumseh Anderson
And with love to Mother, Will

5

The Lord's Prayer

*D*istant tremors and claps of artillery beckoned to the skirmishers, who walked furtively, purposely, fearfully up the slight forest grade toward the crest of the long ridge. They were told to get to the top of the ridge with all due speed, but the top seemed to get farther away, even as the sounds of battle grew louder. The effort was taking its toll as the weary became stragglers who became an unplanned rear guard. The canopy of the lush overhead trees and leaves was cool, too cool for the effort, and the sweat of the foot soldiers dampened the uniform blouses and trousers, chafing the skin, causing shivers and irritation to distraction.

A break in the trees ahead to sunlight beckoned. Drawn to the promise of warmth, heedless of the greater damnation of battle, a fair-haired union soldier quickened his step, suddenly at the head of his skirmish line.

The sunlight met the crest, the top of the ridge, and the trees were gone. Warmth and the far-away shouts of desperation and rifle fire beckoned from an unseen distance. Fair Hair smiled knowing his relief from a heavy wet blouse would soon be met with the arms of the radiant day.

He stepped into the sunlight.

@@@

The enemy's artillery was deadly and effective at almost any range. Only fifty yards away, the worn gun was pointed at the rise of the crest, toward the tree line where the blue coats would emerge. The rebel's junior officer was long dead. A teenage corporal commanded the gun, supervised its loading, and estimated the low arc of its production. He was told days ago that the crest, its abundant trees, and the draw that fed that nearly singular point were his gun's sole mission and target. At this range a direct hit on a man or horse would cause either to explode. Trees and brush ten feet deep would be cut down immediately, or worse, precariously tethered to other trees, now weaker, causing a trap of a wooden avalanche on the unsuspecting. The heat of the projectiles in a single canister, hundreds of pellets, might spark, but most likely would die in the moisture of a forest lush with spring. One spark on tinder wood could start a conflagration.

The rebel corporal thought of his home. He had been hard at it, the fighting and killing and burying the dead, for over two years. Boys came to this isolated lone gun unit, a rear guard, and became fast friends or discounted fools and braggarts, but most were swept away by injury, disease, or desertion. He and four others held this gun position for days on end, their horse long ago taken away by another unit's officer.

They might not be able to escape today. This was their last stand, and each man knew it. The force they heard gasping up the ridge was indistinct but large, and the rebels could be overrun, captured, or killed outright. The corporal had three canisters. He need not allow for cooling; he would load powder, canister, set the breach and fire all three in under a minute, maybe two, in order to draw a reaction. There were only three rifles among the five rebels, and twenty ball rounds with paper and powder. If the blue coats, whether twenty or two hundred, cleared the tree line, the fight was over. The rebels talked of just rapid fire of the canisters, then a hasty retreat toward the main fight to their distant rear. The corporal saw the beauty in this, and it became their plan. Their mission was to delay any force coming up this ridge, through this field.

The gun was ready.

The tops of the trees along the crest line always moved; now the base seemed to shimmer. At the center, precisely where the rebel gun was pointed, a pale face and shock of blond hair emerged, smiling and greeting the sun and sky.

"Fire."

The rebel gun erupted, pointed at a very slight ellipsis for maximum effect of the canister at a few feet above the ground right at the tree line fifty yards away. The gun's flame was frozen for but a moment, orange and white. Heated shot of stones, metal, scrap and smoke and rage burst from the gun and moved through the air in a rolling fury in seconds.

@@@

Fair Hair smiled stepping into the sunshine, never hearing the roar from the rebel gun. He flew back, instantly gone. A twenty foot wide wave of heat and iron hit the forest, weaker and smaller from this position at the crest, and trees started to buckle, splinter, and fall. Several men went down immediately, those who fought to keep up, the strongest and most anxious to secure comfort in the light, while below the crest the slower and the stragglers hit the ground and covered themselves with their hands. No matter how long a soldier had been in battle, had seen death, had brought death, the shock of an artillery canister gave pause and fear became a friend.

Sergeant Kuriger, in command, intoned quickly, "Hurry lads, we've less than a minute. Up and over and charge. From here, on the left, go left, on the right, go right. That gun cannot hit us all. GO."

No hesitation, all hands rushed. Movement can overcome fear briefly, and it was better to attack than wait to be ambushed. The trees at the impact point at the crest were viciously cut, some fallen, many weakened. Safer to leave here and charge the enemy by taking a chance with action rather than the certainty of being crushed by falling trees.

Eighteen to the left, ten to the right. Six stayed where they lay, one groaning and beyond help, the others cruelly but quickly dead. Gunfire slowed, outpaced by hard footfalls in a sprint, heavy breaths gulping in fear and anger and awe.

Sergeant Kuriger led the eighteen to the left, knowing that the sooner they could see the source of the canister explosion, the sooner they could avoid it. A corporal named Perks led the skirmishers to the right. Both groups, running in separate lines no more than two abreast, raced to the opposite tree line, the top of the enfilade of the ridge.

Another canister blew right between the lines, nearly exactly where it had shot previously. No one was hit, but most were knocked off their feet by the concussion, curling or hiding prone even before they hit the ground. One soldier on the right took to his knee after the gun blared, and was shot squarely in the neck, nearly severing his head.

"Get down, stay down," commanded Perks from the right.

Kuriger, on the left, "On me, crawl to the tree line, stay low, keep moving."

Just then a roar of men, close to twenty strong, charged from the right directly into the open field, knowing there was a fight, stepping on Perks' prone squad, charging at a quick step, directly into the line of fire.

Blue coats, all; not Kuriger's unit.

Kuriger barked, "All ye get down, rebels ahead, to your right." The soldiers froze and dropped, accustomed to the voice of command and authority but also accustomed to poor tactical leadership. The rebels opened fire with their rifles, not 20 yards away, cutting down three men, and sheer terror drove the unit to their faces, hugging the low grass, knowing now the charge into the open was pointless, stupid, and suicidal.

A lieutenant among them, very young, shook with the realization of his fatal error. "You heard him, stay down." Too high, fear shaking the words, the pitch lacking authority. The lieutenant suddenly thought the time to move was now, during the rebel reload. He did not calculate the loudness he had heard, of the cannon. "Up now, to the trees."

The rebels had loaded the last canister, and had come upon a cannon ball rusty with time, misshapen and useless for accuracy. The rebel corporal knew that the mass of blue coats, facing in two directions and confused, would recover quickly and overrun them.

"One more round each, when they lift their heads, then run to the bend in the creek below. Fire the cannon. . . now."

The cannon roared.

@@@

"Down, down!" Kuriger bellowed, and to one older private, a rummy they called Rye, who was fearless, "Follow me."

Kuriger dove into the tree line to his left, followed closely by Rye. Sprinting, heedless of whatever he might find, he loosely and rapidly encircled where he guessed the cannon and soldiers were. Kuriger thought there might be only three with the gun, a rear guard not meant to survive a direct assault. Wasting good men because they cannot find a horse to pull the piece, he thought, or the wheels are broken. And at least a dozen good men dead or worse on a hill with no name.

"Halt," this from Rye, who gripped Kuriger's shoulder hard, turned it, and pointed at some dense brush unnaturally flowering in the shade of the forest. Kuriger couldn't see it at first, then, there. The gun, almost on its side, was pointing to the clearing. No rebels there, all gone, and he could hear them crashing down the slope toward what, he did not know.

"Stay here, Rye, don't shoot me." Kuriger hopped and broke through the brush to reach the gun, confident no one had remained to ambush him. Relieved, he darted a few dozen yards away, making noise, knowing that there were still at least three dozen soldiers prone in the field. He was making a grand target for his own frightened soldiers.

"Cease fire, cease fire. The rebs are gone. Stand easy."

The wounded kept moving, the dead and the uninjured were frozen to the earth, the midday heat melting them to the ground. Kuriger walked into the open field.

Of the ten on the right, Kuriger despaired, seeing the one who knelt and was killed by rifle fire, his neck misshapen but face recognizable. Was that a boot print on his chest? Kuriger thought. The rudderless platoon had done it. Of their twenty, ten were dead, cut down by the canister or small arms fire. The young, slight lieutenant sat among five dead men, his own eyes wide, incredulous, running his hands over his head.

"The shot went all around me. I thought I had a few moments before they reloaded." He nearly shouted. "Cannon? What cannon? I was told to secure this ridge, no one told me of cannon!"

The lieutenant's anger overcame his near hysteria.

Kuriger walked up to the boy officer.

"You thought right, about the timing, sir, you didn't know." It made no sense to berate an officer on poor judgment, charging into a clearing, when rage and fear were controlling his actions.

Very softly Kuriger said to the lieutenant, "We should secure the ridge, sir."

The young lieutenant's head snapped and looked hard into Kuriger's eyes, expecting judgment, but seeing an immediate ally.

"What's your name, soldier?" His voice broke.

"Sergeant Kuriger, sir, regular army, H Corps."

"Lieutenant Anderson, Ohio militia. Do secure the hill, sergeant, uh, good work clearing that gun. Should we. . .?"

Kuriger needed to get to work, and could talk to the officer later.

"Rye, take those six," he pointed at men on the far left tree line who had followed him, and were all unhurt, "and set up a perimeter facing outbound. Shout and we'll come running if we get company. Make sure they stay alert."

"Truman, Perks, get a head count. Determine survivors and those in need of attention. Double-quick." Louder, to all in the field: "All hands ensure your weapon is ready to load and fire. Keep it safe unless directly engaged. Bayonets fixed, all."

The six guards under Rye's direction double-timed to respective spots, Rye nudging two to separate more, no *more*, cursing constantly.

Truman checked on men in the field, while Perks went to the opposite tree line to account for the lieutenant's small platoon.

"Let's not forget Easton," said Truman, remembering the fair haired boy.

"You won't. Account for him and the other five where we first entered. Be quick about it," ordered Kuriger, as Truman nodded.

Kuriger looked at the still seated lieutenant. "You have a sergeant here, sir? Who's your non-com?"

The officer pointed at one of the dead, who must have shielded the lieutenant from the cannon blast. The dead sergeant was just a boy, too. His uniform was shredded and filthy, but beneath the blood and dirt there was a newness about the fabric. This sergeant had not been in the field more than a month or two.

"I came into the field with twenty." All the boy lieutenant's men remained either standing or kneeling. None moved to take charge. All stared at the dead sergeant at the officer's feet.

"You have ten dead, sir," said Perks flatly. The ten who rose when you told them to, he thought, just when the cannon opened up. And they shielded you.

"There are four dead over here, sergeant: Miller, Tucker, Garland, and Butler. That's Easton and those five boys from Ithaca back in the trees. You know that." Truman had not intended for the partially suppressed contempt, but there you have it. Dead was dead.

Twenty dead. No major wounds on anyone else, nothing to take a soldier away from duty. Eighteen and six from Kuriger's right flank patrol alive. The lieutenant had ten remaining, including himself. He stared wild-eyed at his dead sergeant. Kuriger expected no direction from this boy officer.

"Perks. Assemble all not on guard. Start digging."

"Right here?"

"Damn right. Right here. Identify, strip valuables and ammunition, take due care. But make haste. The earth is soft, so go down at least four feet. We canna carry them."

The lieutenant's shattered unit started to move, instinctively knowing they were now a burial detail. All had some implement, for digging a small trench was sometimes the difference between living and dying. From a slit trench in the ground you could stay in one spot all day, safe, unless a rebel had high ground on you.

The earth on the ridge was blessedly soft, the fear of minutes before melting into exhaustion from the work. The routine of accounting for and preparing bodies of soldiers for burial was macabre, though soothing. Each deceased was treated as the living would want to have been treated, and a hair's breadth was all that separated the dead and the lucky. Kuriger stepped off what he calculated the length of a trench to bury twenty U.S. soldiers in a mass, now unmarked, grave.

"When you are finished, the lieutenant will say a few words."

@@@

The work went quickly. The muster sheet of those killed and their valuables were in the lieutenant's rucksack. Ammunition was redistributed. The disgrace of twenty dead at the hands of a few rebels with a broken cannon and without firing a shot in response was not lost on Kuriger. He knew some of the older hands were certain of this, too. The young were still dumbstruck by both their failure and good fortune.

Rye walked up to Kuriger, standing too close, smelling of rot and filth. "Haven't heard a sound of anything out there since before you started digging, sergeant."

Kuriger realized, too, that the fight was going away from them, and the farther they were from it the more unlikely the rebels were to capturing them or ambushing again and the safer they would be.

"Lieutenant, we are ready for a proper burial."

Lieutenant Anderson had paced around the perimeter of the ridge since the digging began, unable to reconcile the act of putting his men, his too few men, into the ground forever, without their kin knowing what or how, without a marker on this no name ridge. He struggled for the profound, to talk to God, and found himself nearly weeping. He struggled for the right martial words, and his thoughts were poetic and childish. He struggled to find what a leader would say of this great sacrifice in the face of defeat or victory, and knew he could not come up mute.

"All right, then. Bring the company to attention here," the officer said, pointing to the feet of the uncovered dead.

"Yes, sir." The men, uneven, tired, bleary and broken, slowly came to the mass grave, not quite at attention, but respectful of the importance of the last rays of earthly light to touch on the faces of the deceased.

"Lord, we consign these brave soldiers to Your heavenly arms, in the cradle of Your sweet earth. We pray this was not in vain. We beg Your forgiveness," the lieutenant said clearly, with distinction, "and ask that You welcome these children to sit with You for all time."

Kuriger began, and all followed, "Our Father, Who art in heaven. . ." and all men finished together.

Silence. Truman nodded. Perks said, "Amen." Others said "Amen." And no one moved. Some were rigid, some eyes closed, one cried, most hung their heads. Fatigue was settling into their shoulders, and standing was a great effort exceeded only by moving. One said, "Goodbye." Another, "Rest in peace, brothers."

The wind ran through the tree tops and created a whistle that broke their trance. Birds and bugs made noises that confirmed their solitude. The day cooled.

Kuriger broke the silence after several minutes. "Detail, cover the grave. Well done, gentlemen. Their families would be proud." Mentioning the families helped him. We pray for those who cannot, he thought. "Cover them now. All hands. We need to move shortly."

@@@

Hours later and miles away at the regimental bivouac, young Anderson was standing alone, staring at the quickening sunset, jaw set, teeth grinding together, struggling not to scream. The horses brayed louder than men, he thought, will they not stop? At the edge of a field that tapered down to a slow brook a stone's throw distant, he wanted to lean against the tree beside him, but dared not move as it had taken him too long to stop shaking and get to this point. Other small units converged at the regimental command post with varying degrees of success and failure. All units returned with their wounded, but not all with their dead. Anderson's abysmal land navigation had cost the lives of half his small platoon. He now hid in plain sight, listening to the sounds of camp activity and praying he would be questioned no more today.

Wounded horses were not to be shot. Sergeants instructed the men to cut the animals' throats. The after battle activity was intense though no less horrific than the fight. The lieutenant continued to stare at a fixed point only he could see: his own ineptitude and cowardice.

William Tecumseh Anderson was an officer by virtue of political appointment and education. He had no formal military training, and was forced upon the Ohio regulars as his father was a leader of local militia there, and unable to go to war.

Although the twilight air began to cool rapidly, the lieutenant began to sweat more, and if his jaw was not clenched his teeth would have chattered. Father wanted me to be ready, he thought grimly, fighting back tears. I thought I was ready.

He looked down, kicked a stone, and in the starlit night saw his blood-drenched boot. Another man's blood, from the chest of a private in his command, as young as he, still breathing but ruined with wounds that were fatal yet not quick.

William Tecumseh Anderson ran right over the private, in a full sprint, and looked the near-dead soldier in the eye as his foot found his chest as he passed over. The face of the fallen private showed no pain, no recognition, no judgment of the running officer he had called "Sir, Lieutenant, Sir" cheerfully not one hour before.

Anderson could not shake those two images, the dying private and his father.

@@@

6

Fire

★

*T*here were cloud filled days with bright blue sky and the promise of lazily watching it all pass by. Each dawn would be disquieted by morning sounds of routine, both nature and human. As the day wore on the slowness of garrison life would become sublime as no shots were fired, no entanglement arose, and there might be no fight to survive.

The skirmish lasted but ten minutes, and the casualty count was high. Less than a hundred of both blue and grey ran into the dry high grass of the plateau, surrounded by thick pines dense with growth. The thicket masked sound and point men for respective companies as both armies rushed headlong into the clearing to escape the branches, vines, thorns, and pockets of mud. Barely fifty yards apart, the rebels emerged into the clearing as the noonday sun was at its zenith, nearly twenty abreast, facing due west, while two dozen Yankee infantry charged into the same dry brush, hard at the rebels, facing due east, also unready to fight.

Both charges froze, stared and became dumbstruck, knowing death was near. As union and rebel forces surged behind the soldiers frozen in the sunlight, cursing and hollering for their own men to give way, the Yankee sergeant took charge.

"First squad, take a knee and prepare to fire. Second squad, remain standing and fire at will."

Similar orders were barked by rebel officers, and all kept hollering, all shouting the prelude to attack. Neither company had an advantage, but both thought they had entered an ambush. Tactics differed. The rebel squads that first emerged hit the dry patch of weeds hard, prone, and readied their rifles for the Yankee target oh so close.

The standing Yankees began firing, intermittently, at another company of rebels charging due south into the cleared area. The first rebel volley took five Yankees off their feet, and by now the sergeant had a better assessment.

"Third squad, stay in the tree line where you can. First and second, you will hold your position and maintain fire on that company movement coming south. Third, do not hit our men. Aim with care. Second, take a knee and continue fire."

Several kneeling from this second squad had seen the rebels who were prone firing at them. It was time to engage these soldiers who were hiding too effectively. More union riflemen from the first and second squads were dropping from wounds or kill shots.

The union fire was suppressive on the prone rebels, and the union barrage from the tree line now had the rebel company to the north, now tentatively moving south, halted. At this point over two platoons of union infantry were in the west tree line, afforded tremendous cover but little maneuverability, perhaps seventy strong. The Yankee force had pinned the rebels to the field; the rebels were now all exposed, except for the tall sticks of grass. The rebels would not retreat because they could not retreat. Their climb to the plateau was steep, muddy, demanding, and was still being made even now with stragglers who kept low, beneath the enfilade fire coming from the fight above them.

The union sergeant of the first platoon had decided to try to encircle the open area, moving through the dense brush, toward the north.

A lieutenant came up hard to the sergeant.

"Sergeant Kuriger. That brush to the north is unpassable. There's a culvert maybe twenty feet deep, ten feet at the narrowest point. We'll need to try west and go all around, come up behind."

This lieutenant was a good one, Kuriger thought, grateful it wasn't the boy Anderson, but he thought the route west might take too long. It will be over, he believed, one way or another, in just a few minutes, especially if the rebels had more than those he could account for at the moment.

Kuriger spoke to his platoon. "Sergeant Bearden, take your squad west and north, and come up behind them. Hurry now, double time, fix bayonets, show no quarter." Bearden looked at Kuriger as if he never intended a merciful act under any circumstance, and barked a quick "let's go" to his depleted squad. They moved as one to the west at the run.

"Fire! Brush fire!"

The concentrated rifle fire at the prone rebels caused several sparks on stone or metal or who-knew-what, but a slight wisp of smoke became a wave of flame, the dry grass catching quickly, and the shimmering rush of raw heat and fire fanned out from the eastern point within the clearing.

The screams of terror were sharp, cut short for those rebels prone as the air was whipped away to fuel the flame, taking the screams right out of their lungs. The rebels at the north perimeter of the clearing were unmoved, and the Yankees watching thought the rebs had consigned themselves to die.

The rebels could not move; when two soldiers dove in retreat into the tree line they were met with a vast colony of snakes, fierce, fast and lethal. The copperheads clung desperately to the soldiers who writhed in the mass of muck and slithering reptiles and were wretchedly entangled. The other rebels saw this, turned to the fire racing toward them and then, bedlam.

Some ran to the west tree line, easy prey for the union first and second squads and the remaining platoon amongst the trees. Some rebels began firing into the moving forest floor, fueled now by raw fear, greater than a faceless Yankee enemy.

The fire spread quickly, and would overwhelm the rebel platoon in seconds.

"Cease fire!" First from Kuriger; then, "Cease fire!" from the lieutenant.

The remaining rebels knew instinctively that their only hope to escape a death of snakes or fire was to retreat north to the slope of mud, or charge west away from the fire toward the union troops, and certain imprisonment.

There was little doubt for twenty or so rebels, who dashed frantically with arms aloft to union captors so as not to confuse any intent. The remaining few ran back to the north perimeter, finding safety in the trees.

"Put your weapons down. Sit. Do not move," from an older private to his new prisoners. "Your fight is done."

A rebel officer, young, impossibly young, stood and spoke with high emotion and summoned dignity.

"May I speak with your commander? I have men on that field that may survive. I, we, must attend to them immediately."

The Yankee officer was there already. "You may keep your sword, sir, but all other weapons must be put here," he said, pointing. "You and I will survey the field once the fire has died."

They both looked out at the charred clearing, just moments before a soft golden hue of high grass, untouched by man for at least this season. Now blackened and red, embers dying, no promise of safety.

The rebel officer was shaken and concerned. "We cannot let my men burn to death."

The two enemy officers, heedless of the danger, then ran into the clearing together. At the east end, two rebel soldiers started walking out, and were met by gunfire. One fell, hard, the other grasping a shattered shoulder.

They carried no weapons. The field smoldered and moved.

Damn, the other squad! thought Kuriger. "CEASE FIRE CEASE FIRE."

The two officers continued running across the field, Kuriger armed and close by. They seemed to skim the charred earth, unsure of the risk inherent in the brush fire aftermath but certain of the duty of not allowing a soldier in battle to suffer death by a fire, if it could be helped. They reached the group of prone rebel soldiers. All dead, but one. Kuriger instinctively knelt at his head, turning it. The near expired rebel soldier fired once, point blank, hitting Kuriger's left forearm, shattering the wrist and both bones.

Part Two

Forever

"No trial has come to you but what is human. God is
faithful and will not let you be tried beyond your strength;
but with the trial He will also provide a way out, so that
you may be able to bear it."

1 Corinthians 10:13

7

Surgery

★

*D*r. Tremaine moved purposefully through the parlor-turned-ward, guided by an intense sparrow of a girl, no longer a child, both of them filthy of blood, grease, and sweat. Wounded men lay askew on hardwood boards on the floor, all being attended to by a harried matron fruitlessly trying to keep them in rows, separated, so the doctor could work.

Low indistinct moans peppered the confined space, the sound barely exceeded by the outside buzz of flies cutting through the mid-day air. The ebb and undulation of their presence kept a steady rhythm to their feeding. The smell of excrement, rot, and filth was constant and thick. The doctor stayed to task, checking the wounded in the east-facing parlor of the house, lit only by the softening light from the bay windows, stained with grime. The large open room where two dozen men lay in pain, nearing death, was stagnant. He found it difficult to address the needs of the wounded and dying as fattened flies bit at his own head, neck and hands. He prayed the insects would find more fertile ground to light upon. His instinct for his own comfort he kept to himself. The men in this room would soon die, he thought, better before nightfall, the quicker to bury them.

The quicker to bury them. The west-facing room, the dining area of the house, held those who might make it, though their wounds were grievous. The amputees there were in great pain, but could live. The cries from the wounded were sharper, more distinct than surrounding noises, outraged at missing a foot or an arm coupled with the shock of a life altered forever. Their only succor was that they had survived, had not been consigned to the dead.

The girl hurried to the dining room, with Tremaine in tow. With fewer flies, a chance at relief. He cursed his retreat to self-comfort, but his work with the recovering amputees was more immediate. Six wounded men, side by side on the oversized dining room table, shoulder to shoulder. One was crying; all breathed heavily through gaping mouths, another with eyes clenched, the rest staring at the wood-beamed ceiling as if the abyss.

The doctor looked to the kitchen, directly off the recovery area. Another one, he thought, more soldiers entering there now. Four blue coats burst in, all too young, carrying an out-sized bundle and laying it on the large kitchen table-block, his surgery. The doctor walked woodenly, exhaustion overcoming him now, when adrenaline would have compelled a more able man.

He entered the kitchen and approached the centered block. The four soldiers looked at him anxiously, and then their eyes darted to the girl who entered behind the doctor. She moved quickly, nimble, grabbing uniforms that had been piled on the floor.

"Tear these, quickly," she whispered, intensely, thrusting an armful of rags at the tallest soldier. She darted to the pump, cranked it three times, and spoke to the youngest soldier, nearest the sink.

"Pump these two buckets, then fill any dish you can." The young soldier moved quickly, bumping her hand.

"Sorry, ma'am, missy." A squeak, choked.

"Shush. Just do it now. Wash your hands first, make sure the dishes you use are clean."

The tall one tore rags, while the young one, along with the dirtiest soldier, washed at the pump, alternating gulps of water cupped with their hands. The fourth soldier, closest to the door, heard some silent cry only audible to him, and bolted from the kitchen, hunched over and purposeless.

The doctor looked at the package on the table under the stern gaze of the girl. The package was a boy in uniform, a uniform too big in all respects. The boy's face was pinkish-pale, soft, unconscious. He breathed evenly, though shallow. His forehead and cheeks were gaining some color, a good sign. The jacket was blanketed around the boy's torso, the sleeves rolled so many times they bulged, balloon-like, above his wrists.

The soldier's hands were black with dirt, small, feminine, and frail. His trousers ended in shreds below his knees. Boots, feet, gone. Shins were blood and mud caked and mangled.

"I don't know," the doctor said, thinking, I don't know if I can do one more. The boy might be better off dead. "Perhaps into the parlor."

He prayed silently the girl would agree, take charge again of the soldier detail, and remove the boy, consigning him to his purgatory in the next room.

"No. He has some color. Please, doctor, we need to act now." She would have none of Tremaine's resignation. "Gentlemen, pour water slowly on his lower legs." She began to cut with a carving knife, gently but with dexterity and speed, the trousers above the knee of the first leg, then the other.

"Now slop up the water on the floor with the filthy rags. If you have a clean piece, put it on my shoulder." Young poured in a small stream where directed; Dirty, now kneeling hunched under the table, fought to keep the floor from pooling, finding creases that took the water, blood, and dirt to the crawlspace beneath.

Tall tore rags, dropped the contaminated ones, now looking actively for the clean patches. He embraced the work on the uniforms, seeing a purpose, instinctively moving toward the girl.

Surely she must be protected from this, he thought. And I will protect her. Just as swiftly he reflected, who will protect me?

The doctor came out of his brief fugue state. He kept the blade, a sharpened butcher's tool, above the hutch cabinet behind him. The blade was sharp; the girl kept it that way, always stroking it on a stone immediately after an amputation.

The doctor impulsively thrust the blade under the slow stream of water being poured by Young. The soldier flinched, stopped, then resumed pouring, now over the blade, under the blank gaze of the doctor.

It was sharp. It was clean. It was more ready than he.

The girl plucked a clean piece of cloth from her shoulder, judged it satisfactory for the job, and wound it around a straight large handled spoon from an open drawer of the hutch.

"Not tight enough," she whispered, wound it again, then moved to the head of the table, brushing Tall behind her. She opened the dying boy's mouth, tenderly placing the wrapped spoon handle between his teeth.

"Not yet." The doctor laid the blade down on the broken boy's chest. He wanted to examine the wounds carefully, to make sure the boy had a chance. The left leg, farthest from him, must have taken the first blow. Likely a cannon ball, he thought, probably watched it coming. The speed and friction of the projectile virtually cauterized the wound, causing the complete loss of the boy soldier's lower left leg. Swollen, but even. The water ministrations of Young were effective. The left leg would require no immediate surgery. The knee was intact.

The right leg below the knee was knotted with splintered bone, flesh, uniform, dirt and odd bits of leather and grass. The cannonball must have hit the left leg, and begun to spin and topple the boy soldier in an instant. The ball appeared to have hit the leg from the front, not the side. He must have been running, Tremaine thought, or else he would have fallen backward.

Young, jaw clenched, saw where the doctor was looking.

"More," the doctor breathed into the wound.

Young poured heavily, exhausting the bucket in seconds. "Damn."

Dirty had already filled the second bucket. Handing it to Young, he grabbed the empty bucket and proceeded to pump, grateful for something to do away from the surgery.

"Keep the floor clean after you fill that," the girl stated flatly, and to Tall, she said, "You fill anything you can find." Looking at Tall directly, she whispered, "The doctor will tell you when to hold him down."

The right leg required picking. With precision, as if untying a knot of twine, or freeing a dog from chicken wire, the doctor pulled and coaxed foreign material from the exposed high shin, avoiding bone fragments, marveling at the lack of blood. He picked and pulled with increasing confidence, but stopped suddenly.

Bringing his nose to within an inch of the wound, he snapped at Young, "Stop that."

The flesh behind the leg, the calf muscle and skin had been cut. By a knife, a small one.

Still speaking into the wound, voice raising in question, "Who was with this boy?"

Tall said, "All of us, sir."

"Did you see him fall?"

"Yes, yes I did."

"And?" The doctor needed to know what happened. The boy's condition would not change, but he needed to know if clear thinking prevailed on the field. He saw so little of it; he was impressed. Tremaine stood slowly, creakingly upright.

Tall looked him straight in the eye.

"I saw the cannonball coming, bounding along a dry patch, too late to do anything but jump. Cal jumped, too, only the ball struck a stone and hit him on the rise. When I looked at Cal, his shoulder crashed into my hip. I fell. Cal's head lay on my back. He's been out since."

"Why did it take you so long to get here?" The intensity of battle had ended long before.

"We thought he was dead," from Young.

Dirty stood. Tall looked at the blade on Cal's chest. Said Dirty, "We were hiding."

Tall spat out, "I laid there, face down. I thought Cal might be dead, so I acted dead. But I heard him breathing. I didn't want to look. Seemed like hours." He shook his head slowly from side to side.

Young, near tears, "Everyone was dead. We thought everyone was dead."

"After a time," Tall said mechanically, "the fakers stood, and most ran to the sound of fire. Some ran away. We tended to Cal."

Dirty spread his hands. "That right leg looked like two." He gestured with his fingers clumsily. "We tugged at the boot, and he screamed. We pushed the trouser leg here and there, and saw it, held by, uh, straps, straps of skin."

Young raised his hands to his ears. "When we lifted him, he screamed again. We, we wanted to help . . ."

Tall spread his arms wide, imploring, "And didn't want to go toward the battle. We couldn't move him with the hanging leg. It hurt him, we couldn't carry him right."

Tall sighed heavily, looked at the girl, then he looked beseechingly at the ceiling.

"I took my knife, and cut through the skin against a rock. Cal never said a word. We stopped the bleeding with a . . . found jacket. We brought him here when the guns stopped."

Tall, Young, and Dirty stared at the doctor. Young flinched at an imagined irritant.

"Good job. He'll live." The doctor put his nose back to the right leg wound.

"But the knee is lost."

@@@

After the surgery, the doctor and the girl stood over the sink, she pumping the water for him.

"Papa? The flies go to the dead quickly. Can we keep horse carcasses downwind from the house, away from the privy? Perhaps draw the flies?"

He thought that discarded limbs might serve better, and smell less. "No, Delaney, we'll keep the animals away if we can. The army will keep the dead horses separate from the working horses. They must." Both silently understood that the dead brought insects which brought disease and eggs and more insects, and that a shallow water supply could be quickly contaminated. Disease with the soldiers was already rampant. More died from infection and illness than anything else.

Such a waste, Tremaine thought. Horses are my living, and I must ignore them. God meant for men to be treated first. Sometimes ungrateful men. Better some be treated like wounded horses. These soldiers kill each other, neighbors, and have no respect for themselves, for their lives. Ah. I will keep to myself. Cannot lose all over the war of vain men.

"We must protect our ranch, Delaney. I'll raise more horses. Later, when this ends."

"Your work has been good, papa. You have saved lives. All the men in the dining room would have died without you."

@@@

Tall, Young, and Delaney carried Cal to the dining room, after they had washed. The doctor had examined the six men on the table, and found one had died, choking to death on his tongue and spittle. Dirty was instructed to take the corpse outside immediately. The dead soldier was hoisted over Dirty's shoulder, and carried out the front door, down the porch steps, and to the road for the army's recording of the passing.

Dirty laid him down gently, starting a new row behind a long line of dead, their feet facing the wide hard-packed clay path. He said a short prayer, gaped at the line of corpses, and closed the eyes of the dead soldier, forcing the jaw shut, tilting the head to face the graying light of the late day sky. Rigor had yet to set in. The soldier did not look at peace; his expression was agonized, even in death, even though his soul had passed into the arms of the Lord.

The arms of the Lord. This dead man had no arms. I'd swallow my tongue and puke to death, too, thought Dirty. The man had no arms. Dear God, he thought, I don't know if I can do this any more.

In the house the table was full again. Cal rested fitfully on the end. Delaney whispered to him, a mixture of pity, sweetness and anger, softly murmuring into his hair at the crown of his forehead.

The doctor waved the soldiers to the east facing parlor room. "Time to thin our ranks, boys. Buck up."

Dirty walked back into the house, stepped into the postoperation dining room, and sensed no movement. He thought he saw the girl kissing Cal's forehead, gently, feather-like, prayerful, silently weeping. At least Cal was not alone.

"In here," said Tall. The doctor was checking the wounded, shoulder to shoulder, in two rows on the parlor floor. Men awaiting their end, but not on their terms. Most were unconscious. Starting at the place to start, thought Young, right here.

At the third man, Tremaine crossed the soldier's arms and closed his eyes.

"Take this man out."

Tall bent and started to hoist.

"No, carry him as you would your brother. His journey is over. May God have mercy on his soul."

Dirty took charge, and he and Tall lifted the dead soldier and took him outside to join the line by the dirt path. Young began to shake, chilled in the heat, feverish but cold, frightened by flies and the stench.

"Delaney," the doctor barked, "Delaney."

The girl flew into the room, slipping on waste and fluid on the hardwood floor that had not seeped through. She caught herself as Young did, and pushed herself away from him. Young did not intend to grope, only to prevent her from falling. His grips on her were all wrong for due care, all amazing for the promise of his manhood to be, and all woman.

"Sorry, Dee, miss, sorry."

"Shut up, boy." She elbowed her way, gliding and stomping, graceful and sure, to the doctor's side, her long skirt hanging like a blanket tapestry.

"Does this man look better to you?" The doctor was looking curiously at the wounded soldier, an older man, who he thought had already bled out. His color was higher, what the doctor could see of it. The soldier's face was scarred, dark and heavily bearded. Even in repose his bearing was unmistakable. The wounded soldier coughed, phlegmatically from his chest, dryly from his lips.

"He's choking," whispered Delaney. She turned his head and stuck the fingers of her right hand into his mouth, while her tiny fist screwed between the soldier's jaws. One tooth dug deep.

"Careful, dear." The doctor forgot why the soldier was in this purgatory room. No fever. No head or neck or wound in extremis. Hands and feet intact. Hands. The left hand was grey and slack.

Delaney said, "He's okay now." She sucked quickly at the hole in her knuckle, then wiped it on her hip.

"Gunshot through his left forearm. I thought he had bled out."

"Yea, God. The sergeant." Young knelt at the wounded man's feet.

"He's our Company First Sergeant, Sergeant Kuriger. He led the first charge. Can we help him? He aren't dead, right?"

"He isn't dead, and we can help him." Tremaine couldn't tell Young that he thought the sergeant dead because his breathing was too shallow, and color too poor, only hours before. When the doctor tried to bring this sergeant to surgery, earlier that day, Kuriger had gripped his arm with a massive right hand, growling in a menacing voice fraught with danger and its own promise.

"Don't cut my arm off. Swear it."

The doctor had whispered, frightened by this soldier, that he wouldn't.

"I swear."

At that the sergeant had passed out.

He will die, thought Tremaine, and I swore to let him die.

Tall and Dirty entered the room. Young rose his timid voice above the din of the flies and the stink of death, "It's Sergeant Kuriger; he's alive!"

@@@

It was night. Kuriger now lay on the table next to Cal. He breathed deeply, evenly, resigned. He was overwhelmed with hunger and thirst. Turning his head to his left, he looked at a credenza, deep red wood, with painted spring flowers in whirls around the cabinet handles. A knot marred the chest, near the center door seam, cracked and caved, about the size of an egg. It winked at him in the lamplight. The cabinet maker had painted a canary-like bird approaching the flaw, the knot. Its curiosity arrested his gaze. The bird seemed to be in mid-flutter, whether alighting on the knot or inspecting it, Kuriger was unsure. The painted scene gave the credenza a beauty greater than the original wood, and seemed to make the piece unlevel. Atop the credenza were two candles and three wooden angels, all tall, lean, sparse and functional. The angels balanced the credenza, and he thought he had never seen as pretty a piece of wood carved by man. It was beautiful for its endurance, the artist's eye capturing the flaw and making the credenza magnificent.

Kuriger's left arm was pained. He made fists with his hands, feeling his strength coming back, conflicted by his hunger and thirst. Good, he thought, he didn't cut off my arm. He could feel everything, especially his hunger. A good sign. His pain was acute, he hurt everywhere, but a long draught of water and he would be on his way.

He turned to the right. A boy soldier was awake next to him, gulping for air, sobbing. He stared at the boy; he knew him. Part of the company. Eager lad, quick to please. A good soldier, if he could survive. Kuriger was committed to the survival of the young soldiers. They wanted to do their duty, honor bound, and took instruction very well, respectful of experience.

His hunger distracted him, his thirst was intense. He tried to tongue his loose tooth, as the action usually generated saliva. His tongue was too swollen, but he knew the tooth was there; it hurt like hell. As he fought to find the tooth, smells began to register. Sweat, mud, horsecrap, his crap, blood oh God the blood, and the ever present hum of the flies.

"Stop it," he croaked, "Stop that sound."

Kuriger almost fell back to sleep, but he instinctively knew to stay awake. His cry for the noise to stop went unheeded. His tongue was becoming moist, but the taste was too bitter. His thirst was slaked by a cut on his tongue, the tooth found now and the pain of this rawness and the slipperiness of his mouth and lips were too tempting in pleasure to stop.

His throat worked itself. He ached, too much to sit up.

"Sergeant Kuriger?" The boy spoke to him, red-eyed, puffy, and struggling to be brave.

Private Straw, yes. Good boy. Able lad.

"Straw," his old voice began to come back. "How are you, soldier?" Kuriger turned his head to him.

"My legs are gone, I think, I have no legs, I have no legs." Cal turned to face the ceiling, his voice and spirit trailing off.

"Let's have a look." Kuriger rose on his right elbow to face Cal Straw. The boy was beyond morose. Kuriger's heart began to rage, head pounding. He turned his hips toward Straw, and moved his left arm across his body toward the boy.

Kuriger's left arm was gone at the elbow. Impossibly swollen, red, sutured with, what? Bandaged, dried blood caked, some weeping at one point.

Kuriger stared at his arm stump. He made a fist. He felt it, felt his fingers work and move. It wasn't there.

"I'll kill that doctor for all of us."

"Dear God," said Straw, "I have no legs."

"But you're alive, both of you." Delaney floated into the room and brought in cool moist rags and compressed one on Straw's head. "Shush, shush, please sleep.

"And you will kill no one today, sergeant," she said evenly to Kuriger. "Now lay down and let me check your wound."

"Water first. I canna think."

Delaney set the bowl and rags on the credenza, pushing the angels farther back toward the wall. She darted into the kitchen and returned immediately, holding a large cup of water.

"You must lay down, sergeant, I'll lift your head."

"No, I'll sit."

Still on his elbow, facing Straw, the absurdity of not being able to grip a cup and drink was almost comical. He shifted his hips to the left, but misjudged his purchase of the table top. His left arm shot with pain, his elbow stump much too tender for a fulcrum. His heart thudded, head exploded, white hot. Kuriger bit down rather than cry out, gouging his tongue. He tipped over the edge and the floor rushed to him.

Prone, confused, in pain and angry, he grunted heavily and stayed still.

"He swore he wouldn't."

"Are you, are you alright?" Delaney still held the cup, fearful for the sergeant's abrupt fall, but more frightened by what he might do when he stood.

Kuriger had caught himself with one knee, his right forearm, and his face. He shook his head, turning it toward the credenza and Delaney's voice.

"I am fine. Just give me a moment." His anger was acute, but this child only wanted to help him. It was not her fault, this war, Straw's missing legs, his arm. Kuriger looked at the credenza, and now the bird loomed just over his head. The yellow bird was sparrow-like, a soft maize, the imagination of a long forgotten cabinet maker. Its eye was most intense. Yes, he thought, she's inspecting the knot, the flaw. And she doesn't approve.

"Help me up." Relieved, Delaney knew the storm had passed. Her concern for Straw was overwhelming, yet this beast's thirst must be slaked.

Kuriger knelt and steadied himself, extending his right hand, a commanding gesture.

Delaney quickly complied, handing him the cup. "Easy," she said.

Kuriger drank it down quickly. "More, more, please."

Dirty entered. "Sergeant, are you okay? I heard a crash. I'll help you."

"Stand easy, Dobbs. I don't need your help. Just more water. Straw first." Kuriger spat blood. "Damn," he mumbled, and thought, I really cut the heck out of my tongue.

Delaney reentered with two cups, handing one to the still kneeling Kuriger, who poured it down quickly, again, thrusting it back to Dobbs and nodding with authority for more.

Delaney lifted Straw by the shoulders, bringing the shallow cup to his lips. "Drink slowly." Much dribbled on his chin. The soldier to Straw's right awoke with a start.

"I smell water," he croaked. His mouth was numb with dirt, like a hard packed road. "Gimme some."

Cries for water started slow, and rose. The other men on the table, grimy, sweaty, addled by pain, begged for water. Dobbs brought in a bucket, filled, and Delaney scooped and helped, scooped and poured, scooped and dribbled for the men. They could not get enough. As their thirst was satisfied, their pain edged away, and the enormity of their changed lives came rushing upon them.

"My leg."

"My arm."

"My hand."

"My God."

8

Thunder

*P*rivate George Huntred was always big, bigger than his shoes, his clothes, his tools, his tent, his friends and everyone in his company. Biggest of all was his laugh, like thunder, which equally frightened and struck soldiers with awe. His guffaws, once unleashed, barked to the heavens, becoming the fire of a thousand sparks of the banal and the bawdy. Being near Thunder, as he was called as long as he could remember, meant you were in on the joke, and since Thunder loved his own laugh, it was always better to fuel it than suppress it.

And this Thunder was gentle, so averse to the pain of others that in eight months in the field, in over ten serious engagements with the enemy, he had yet to fire his weapon. For the first two battles, he had managed to load shot and powder four times in his rifle, sweating and spitting and hollering rage to mask his fear. I've never shot so much as a rabbit, he thought; I can never shoot another man, or boy, smaller than me.

After the second battle, an officer took note that his weapon appeared not right. A quick inspection, furtive glances, accusations, and denial followed. George stated accurately that his weapon was jammed and he just kept at it, thinking it might suddenly work.

"I don't know how to clear it, sir, I can't explain it."

The officer could see the dilemma. Accusing the giant soldier who had stood his ground and never fired a shot would be unproductive. Coddling fear was worse.

"Sergeant, find a position for this soldier with a forward battery. They could use a strong back."

The sergeant kept his smile hidden. "Yessir. If a mule gives out, Private Huntred can take its place."

For the next several months through eight significant contacts with the rebels, Thunder did the work of three men and a horse. A strong horse. The battery gun he was assigned to had distinguished itself in its ability to position quickly, in no small measure to Thunder's power and endurance. Coupled with a junior officer's training in gun placement and declination preparation and azimuth direction, that artillery piece was the jewel of the battalion.

Bravery can be measured by obedience to fundamental and repetitious tasks that are boring, menial, and simple enough for even the feeble-minded, and which sometimes appear to the untrained as easier than it actually is in practice when performed under fire and extreme duress. In the face of rifle fire, mortar bursts, and artillery fragmentation and concussion, the routine tasks of a soldier become death defying and heroic. Thunder and the men of Gun Two were the bravest of the brave, never thinking to take solace in the plain fact they rained death, but never saw its effect. Thunder never had to look another man in the eye before he killed him, but he knew his actions did kill, and kill many. It brought him no comfort.

So that others may live, he thought. I, too, want to live. These soldiers with me want to live, honorably; so we stand our ground, do our work.

The men of Gun Two never considered that once they were engaged, there was little room for cover and concealment. The men of Gun Two could not hide. Other artillery pieces around them took hits from the enemy, devastating cataclysms of fire and shrapnel and gore, and Gun Two remained unscathed for half a year.

Thunder was his name, now not for laughter, but as the identifying soldier of a gun that always achieved its mission in the face of calamity and brutal attrition.

Moving the guns was sometimes worse than the fight. In battle, there was an inevitability of consequence: clear, load, check, aim, fire, sight effect on target, adjust, repeat; drilled cadences and the process of manipulation to be counted out loud, without failure. It was by the book for artillery, up to a point. The battery's guns had yet to be attacked by enemy infantry. The gunners and ammunition haulers had yet to fight hand to hand.

But moving the guns. Backbreaking, especially in mud, and both men and horses could be spent after less than an hour's work secured only thirty feet uphill. Except for Thunder, who never seemed to tire. He grew stronger under exertion, oblivious to rest and the idleness of waiting. Like three men and a horse, they said; perhaps, three horses in one man.

Spring rains wreak havoc on dirt roads, and the weight of the guns created grooves that sank the carriages to the center of the wagon-wheels. Putting Gun Two in front helped, as the effort to keep up by the other guns was positive. The soldiers had devised a system of using wooden lids of ammunition boxes as hand held ramps to prevent the wheels from sinking too deep, and as an afternoon tactic, as the ground began to dry, it was effective. On an unusually warm winter's day in 1864, headway was being made, Gun Two at the lead, and the column was halted to rest.

Rest for the horses. The men were restless. Thirsty, exhausted, dizzy from exertion, they wanted to be on their way. The soldiers were told there was two hours of smooth march on even terrain in front of them, then bivouac and hot food and sleep. The officers were so confident of the battery column's security, they granted permission for the anxious but now grateful soldiers to smoke. There would be much work to do and miles to make before they bedded down for the night.

Tobacco was shared, pipes and paper, and for several long minutes there was little talk, just smoke. It hung in the dry windless afternoon air, the trees providing a bounty of shade and coolness. Horses were absently watered, as were the men, and a stout sergeant called easily but firmly, "Prepare to march."

Thunder never knew who was careless that day. A spark, a lit match to rekindle a dying pipe, a cigar stub not stripped. He supposed an ember was tossed and misdirected, landing on an open box of gunpowder in the short carriage behind Gun Two.

They heard the fizzle first, unmistakable in its lethal potential. A thread of black smoke rose straight up in a line and instinctively all hands but one dove to the dirt or berm or fallen log to escape the explosion that would devastate everything in its path outwards and upwards.

Thunder moved quickly to the hiss and fizzle, canteen open and ready, throwing precious water ahead of him, thinking the horses would surely die just standing there.

A flash, a fire, then white hot light. A rumble underneath the carriage, then nothing; no sounds.

"Jesus, get some water on that now, save what powder you can. And put out those damn pipes," from a young officer.

"That was close," the stout sergeant said. "No explosion, no carriage damage we can't fix. Anyone hurt?"

Thunder was flat on his back, head ringing, barely making out the questions around him. He tried to blink, thought he might be dreaming. The sounds became more distinct; he rolled to his side, and took one knee, running his hands on his chest, stomach, groin. Then he touched his face. Too wet, he thought, I'm not sweating any longer. He was awake, alert, and the sounds around him were louder, sharper and then the hands of others were on him, pressing bandages on his face, his eyes.

"His eyes are torn up, and the gash on his forehead won't stop, but it's just a gash," from a private on the same gun.

"Huntred, Thunder, can you hear me?" from the sergeant.

"I hear you," he croaked. He tried to bow his head, the enormity sinking in, but all those hands held him steady, staunching the flow of blood.

"Ye God. I'm blind."

@@@

9

Grant, Spring 1864

★

*T*he General's tent was spacious but spartan. He was conscious of how he would look to his men, not just privates and bounty men, but to the officers around him, those staffers who performed admirable work in administration, logistics and even publicity, yet had never fired a weapon in anger or fear. Nor had they been directly fired upon.

It is better that these soft staffers not see any more glamour in this war, he thought; it is better that they feel a hunger for good things. They'll be more inclined to end all this than perpetuate it.

He ate sparingly, not much different than the field ration of his army. His army. They moved better this year, under his guidance and control. The intensity of his leadership was less pageantry and more brutal, more martial. He demanded that every man, jack, and child engage the enemy, and above all, pursue. It was the lack of this pursuit that permitted Lee's army to strike and maneuver, moving with impunity through Virginia and Maryland. He thought of that audacity of Lee entering Pennsylvania last July. Just butchery.

But butchery, General Grant knew, would be the only way to end this war.

The siege at Vicksburg and the fight along the Mississippi were tremendously productive, though faintly immoral. He was willing to starve the enemy, deny food and supplies to fellow Americans who saw their way of life as more important than the nation, the law, or human dignity. How one man could own another man, rationalize that behavior, and stand behind the name of God at the same time brought his blood to boil. It would not stand. So they would starve. This was their doing, not his. Grant was committed to end it. Quickly and brutally, if necessary. It would be immoral to not end it.

Brutal he would be. No remorse, no pity, and no quarter. The general knew that complete surrender was necessary, and without overwhelming suffering the rebel cause would never yield. Unless Lee and his army were brought to heel, or annihilated, the war would never end.

The general was trying to write a letter to his wife. He struggled with the attempt to sound nonchalant, knowing that she would see his effort as commendable but false. He stared at the blank paper, hand frozen, pen drenched in ink, ready to write but unable.

"General Grant."

"Yes." That intense captain, Hendricks, the one with all the ideas.

"General, Colonel Time is here, sir, you wished to speak with him."

"Give me a moment, captain."

Grant started to put the pen away, and decided against it. He set it down and looked through the tent flap. Captain Hendricks was staring at him, mouth slightly agape, eyes very intense. The general marveled at the incongruity, knowing that Hendricks possessed a first-rate mind; alas, the very beauty of his numerous flashes of brilliance guaranteed a few random and crazy exhortations, but this time, oh, this time he has struck a deep chord. Grant looked toward the waiting Colonel Time, and smiled inwardly as Time gazed out at the sunset. The colonel had served with him out west, with great distinction. Time was brave, mature, exercised consistent good judgment, was a slave to Army regulations and enjoyed whiskey. A model officer.

Time could have been a general, Grant thought, but his injuries were too grave. Time's body was beginning to succumb to the savagery of war. The colonel never shirked his responsibility to lead his men, really lead, from the front, and narrowly escaped death several times. The compounded wounds over the past two years were catalogued by everyone in his command. Loss of an eye at Bull Run. Three fingers of his left hand at Chancellorsville while shielding a wounded soldier from a maniacal rebel officer flaying wildly with his sword; Time's fingers flew off, and then he buried his personal knife, all ten inches of it, into the rebel's abdomen.

Right knee ineffective and Achilles tendon of the same leg ruptured, both irreparably. He walked with a wide but steady gait. He could not walk too far without rest and could not mount a horse without assistance. On most occasions he used a cane or walking stick.

Grant knew, also, that Time's hearing was fading fast, and that his head and hand shook on their own volition. The whole regiment knew.

One of my finest regimental commanders, and now I have to relieve him, he mused. A whiskey will soften the blow. Maybe two. And Hendricks's idea may benefit us all.

Grant smiled. That officious staffer Hendricks hit upon a profound solution to free more valuable resources with an invalid corps on the move, not just around Washington.

"Captain Hendricks, please show the colonel in."

Time strode directly to Grant, not acknowledging Hendricks. He saluted, and Grant returned it by standing and extending his hand and smiling.

"Good to see you, Colonel. No formalities in this tent. It is very good to see you. Please sit." They shook hands quickly.

"May I stand, sir? I am more comfortable standing," the lie came easily, sounded sincere, and Grant allowed it with a nod.

"I'll sit, Colonel, if that's okay with you. May I offer you a refreshment? Please join me." Grant poured one whiskey, looked at the agitated Time, who, with a sharp intake of breath, nodded affirmatively.

Grant poured with a soft smile, handing a rough hewn glass to Time, just the right amount. Enough for a man in pain to enjoy.

"Thank you for joining me in my evening respite, Jon. I would have hated throwing you the hell out of here."

Hendricks laughed on cue, and Time grinned appreciatively. "Thank you, general, it has been too long since. . ."

Grant raised his glass. "To the United States."

"The United States," Time said dutifully. They drank as if alone.

The silence initially was between two violent men, whose hardened hearts let the liquor bathe their thirst. Silence between friends who had seen death, brought death, shared death, and had survived. Silence of a hundred stories untold, a thousand histories, and the common thread of savage leadership in desperate times connecting them. Grant's eyes were closed. Time stared down at the floorboards of the command tent, and slowly raised his head level, looking squarely at the general.

"Am I to be relieved, sir?" Time's only fear was disgrace, to leave the field alive while his men were still engaged, and without complete victory. He began to shake, controlling a slow building rage.

"No. But I have a reassignment for you."

"That's the same damn thing, sir, and you know it. Begging your pardon, general, my regiment has seen much, fought well, and I cannot leave the field now, when victory is so close."

"This is a crucial assignment, Jon."

Time shook his head, and looked at Hendricks, and took a step toward him.

Hendricks flinched as if stricken, stepping back.

Grant laughed, "Now, now, colonel, beating the hell out of a staff captain will not change things. I am giving you command of a newly formed regiment."

Time froze. He slowly turned his head toward the general, though remained poised to advance on Hendricks for some indefinable reason.

"General, did you say a new regiment?"

"Yes, colonel, this is a new concept on a current regulation. Captain Hendricks has the details."

Hendricks launched into his prepared remarks.

"Colonel, the Invalid Corps was created last year as a method to keep the crippled in service, chiefly in defense of Washington. After some fits and starts, we saw a need to rename the regiment into the Veterans' Reserve Corps, with standard issue uniforms. Within five miles of this location there are over a thousand unassigned and injured soldiers who can provide service, freeing up the fully capable for field duty. All are volunteers, of course. Any man missing a limb is not required to stay in service. But these men want to be of use. Right now the able-bodied, whether conscript, bounty or volunteer, are being used to guard supply trains, warehouses, prisoners, and newly mustered recruits. Cripples can do the job. Cripples want to do the job."

Time interrupted. "Veterans. You do mean veterans, captain. They know they're cripples, we need not call them that."

"Of course, Colonel Time," Grant waved his hand. "You are right."

Hendricks continued. "We have enough men in the vicinity to make up two battalions. The first will be men with injuries of limited amp. . ." Hendricks hesitated, stared at Time's left hand, coughed, and plowed ahead when the storm cloud stamped on Time's face passed without threat.

"Limited amputations. Mostly healing broken bones, and some with wrenched backs or bad legs. All in the first battalion are ambulatory, effectively ambulatory. The second battalion has more grievous injuries. They would be assigned less rigorous duty, perhaps standing watch while seated, riding gun on a supply wagon through suspected marauder territory. There are many possibilities."

Time, now seated, knew his fate. Relieved of command in the field, and without the satisfaction of death or victory, he would now be a nurse for crippled veterans. His own limitations forced it. But it was better than being retired.

Time stretched his neck back, taut, "Captain. . ." Hendricks cut him off.

"Colonel, the uniforms last year were robin's egg blue, for distinction. The general thinks that regulation uniforms should be maintained, unless you think otherwise, preferring the light blue."

Time glared. Hendricks was spared by Grant. "Captain, let's digest this. The colonel has an observation."

"Thank you, sir," Time said to Grant. "I believe that motivated men can do anything, and the motivation of injured men can be very compelling, indeed. I do request to meet each man, sir; the power of hate could make this adventure ill-advised. If such a regiment is to remain on the march, it will have to do more than stand guard. It will drill. Soldiers with all their faculties sleep restlessly enough, and are quick to anger. The wounded man is prone to lash out in the absence of orders, by whatever means is at his disposal."

Time paused, and stated distinctly, "I must be given wide authority to accept or deny any man in this regiment."

"Of course, colonel," said Grant, flatly.

Hendricks wisely, with great effort, kept silent.

"Thank you for the opportunity, general." Time finished his drink in one swallow, set the glass down, and rose to attention, saluting smartly, staring into an unseen distance, rigid and professional.

Grant stood also, and sharply returned Time's offer of respect.

"Who replaces you, Jon?"

Time was cut to the quick. He had not expected to be asked. His immediate concern now was that his executive officer would be given command, which would be an error. His second-in-command was a most capable logistician and general tactician, but his strength was not fighting warfare.

The man could move ammunition, supplies, food and horses with great skill, but he was not suited to move men to fight.

"This is unexpected, sir. If I may, I have a junior officer, a captain," glancing slyly at Hendricks, "named Brown, who is a good leader under fire. His men and peers respect him. May I respectfully request that he be appointed as regimental commander? He's not a kid, general; he's a college professor of Latin and Greek, I believe, from New York, Buffalo. Nearly thirty. He, uh, has whiskers." A smile now, and a look at Hendricks, who appeared years away from a razor.

Grant looked at Time. He's testing me, dammit, and he's got me. "I don't know this Brown. . ."

Hendricks coughed, nodded once, jaw set, and looked imposing in judgment, staring at Grant.

"Well," said the general, "Brown it shall be. I'll speak with him in the morning. I was wondering, colonel, if you would like to take a walk? Perhaps visit some of your command, maybe a few hands of poker?"

It was difficult for Time to hide his astonishment. His natural infantry contempt for staffers was shattered when he saw the deference Grant afforded Hendricks's judgment on Time's replacement. And for the general to walk with Time through the regiment's bivouac, comrades taking a stroll, would soften his relief of this crucial command, and heighten Time's stature and his men's morale.

"I would be honored, sir. Allow me to lead the way."

Hendricks darted through the tent and gestured to two soldiers standing guard. "Follow the general and the colonel at a discreet distance. Protect them at all costs. I will move ahead of them. Keep me in sight. Try to steer them my way." Hendricks knew where Time's men were tonight. He knew where all of Grant's command was located. He knew his own weakness, the fear of fire on the battlefield. He knew his own strength, keeping the General of the Army informed. He strode purposefully toward a fire ringed with soldiers in the distance.

Grant and Time emerged from the command tent.

"Your young captain moves quickly. And I can see why you trust his judgment," Time smiled.

"He has a good head, and I know he has no political dog in the fight, so to speak. Every now and then a 'robin's egg' comment flies off his tongue, and. . ."

Both soldiers laughed, enjoying the night air, comfortable in and burdened by their chosen profession, eager to talk to their troops. They walked into the darkness, toward a flickering fire, a lonely captain at their lead, whose nervous intelligence gave urgent orders to those in his path to stand easy but ready. The general and the colonel are walking through, they've heard you have performed with honor of late, and want to make certain that you know they know.

Grant slowed his walk pace to match Colonel Time, the new commanding officer of the Veterans' Reserve Corps, the 18th.

@@@

My dearest, I have little time to write, and much to tell you. I think of you and the children constantly and pray for your good health. I know the Lord is watching over you. I would be mad with worry if you were not in your father's care. I have received your daily letters, though not quite daily, and my joy at reading and reading again each word cannot be described except my heart aches for you and our children.

Young Jon sounds as if he is ready to venture out in the world. I recall much of how I saw life at age seven. The boy is headstrong like my brother, James. Andrew is the apple fallen not far from the tree. I trust his restless silent nature will bring honor to our household. I have tried to make my life around that prospect. Please kiss my angel girls, dearest, they so favor you.

My injuries are slight enough. I am grateful that I am able to retain a command. The 18ᵗʰ is a professional unit, and is now my life's work to lead, God willing.

I allow my fate into His hands, and your prayers. I cannot allow my fate to alter others wrongly.

*I remain your devoted husband, father to the finest genera-
tion of beauty and love and faith,*

All my love, Jon

10

Duty

★

*T*he formation of the 18th Veterans' Reserve Corps under
Colonel Jon Time was smooth logistically, partly because
there were no conscripts; all volunteered. As the word spread
that wounded, invalid soldiers could expect an honorable
workday, paid, and in standard uniform, there was little hesitation. Those who wanted to join did. Those who wanted to go
home were understood, without remonstration or judgment.
A good amount tried to talk their comrades out of joining
the 18th, seeing the injuries of others as always more severe
than their own. The decisions of some teetered on a soldier's
destination: the comfort of an accepting home, family who
could welcome and nurse and love, or the abyss of no future,
a trade no longer possible, a lack of friends or the strain of a
life of pity and silent scorn. A man in the army was a laborer,
and the lack of a hand, a leg, or more prevented the prospect
of a gainful future. A man's life could not pivot on a second
chance when fate spared his life but stole his livelihood.

The farmer without sons must return to his homestead
simply to rent or sell his land. With sons he could try to make a
go of it. With daughters he could dowry his land. The decision
of the farmer was made by his wife or his woman, a strong
figure cut from the earth who could see survival and guide a

family to a better fortune. This citizen-soldier could only see as far as the end of his arm or leg, the gnarled stump, the constant pain, knowing he would never drive a plow, or a team of horses, or swing an axe or catch and butcher an animal again.

For the love of God he could not eat or bathe or relieve himself without help.

Some of the breathing were already dead. The formation of the 18th was the thin tether of hope that could keep an able but invalided man alive.

Academics, lawyers, the educated in general went home. Their skill was their heads and tongues. The laborer stayed and was the foundation of the 18th. These men were the strongest of the strong, forged in battle, backs attuned to the stress of hard work, boys who became men awash in fatigue, self-reliant from their first consciousness.

And soldiers they wanted to be.

@@@

The formation of the 18th Veterans' Reserve Corps was not without its own fanfare and foolishness, encouraged by curious Washington, D.C., townsfolk exhausted from war, politicians and their ilk at arm's length, and drums of all sizes.

A crippled man can bang a drum, a dissonance of useless time marked. Marching drill to a drumbeat with invalids was sometimes unproductive but had a bellicose air. The irregularity of drumbeats heightened the anxious commitment of the corps, and its mission to guard confederates, bounty men, and supplies. Standards of the watch would be loosened to accommodate those who needed to sit on duty, and pairs were organized within squads to complement skill, a term of deception that detracted from the naked truth: a pair of guards required one soldier who could load and fire a weapon unaided.

An unspoken tenderness develops between the roughest of men when one is touched by God to assist, no matter how difficult or routine the task may be. The volunteer veterans of the 18th knew their individual purpose in life was bound by their humanity to each other, even in the face of their own crippling injuries.

And odd couples they made.

Musgrove and Messerel respected and trusted their physical differences and complementary skills. Musgrove, bony, tall, bucktoothed with a wild shock of black hair, lost his left leg a year before, outside Fredericksburg, with the 150ᵗʰ Pennsylvania. Four soldiers had died around him, concussed by cannon fire, untouched otherwise. His left foot had become infected, so they cut off his toes. The gunk deepened, painful, and crept to his ankle. The surgeon took off the leg at the knee, many inches above the last trace of infection. It took months to heal, and in that time Musgrove worked his hands, arms, and back, now possessing shoulders like cannon balls. He squatted or sat duty at the regimental hospital for over half a year, since before Christmas, until he was assigned to the 18ᵗʰ. Units came and went, soldiers died, and many of those uninjured did not look him in the eye. Musgrove had family to return to, yet his wound came not from battle but from an ill-fitting shoe, a small stone wedged against his skin and nail, and the heat and sweat and friction of it had nearly killed him.

Musgrove would not go home without his leg just because his socks were poorly made. He would help where and when he could. He took his own rations after the sick, stood for officers and managed an unbalanced salute, and tipped his cap to women, endearing himself to the nurses as a gentleman. One in particular, a chubby girl named Sheila, always brought him butter, real butter, with bread every morning. He slept on the porch at the door of the infirmary, a self-imposed sentry, and for six months no one challenged him or his authority, and he sighted his rifle when he could, cleaned it often, and even sharpened his bayonet.

Musgrove wanted to be ready. He had no chance as yet to be a hero. Young Sheila was in awe of her strong soldier, though she never managed more than a "good morning."

Messerel joined the 18ᵗʰ boiling with anger.

He lost his right arm to the elbow trying to retrieve his cap in the mud, before it was run over by a supply wagon. The march that day had started uneventfully. The horses were moving uphill, Messerel next to the train, all moving at a slow and steady pace. While wiping his brow, a gnat entered his eye, he jerked his head, and his cap fell into the path of the rear wheel. Messerel knew he had time to pick it up and flicked his hand to grasp it.

The horses lurched, the ground was not thick, and the wheel skipped a rock and rolled on his hand. Messerel hollered, the driver halted, the wheel firmly planted and crushing his wrist, rocking slightly back and forth and back and forth. He shrieked himself unconscious.

Messerel woke in the infirmary days later, right hand gone. Broad shouldered, barrel chested, ruddy dark and light of eyes, dear Lord, he thought, my right arm. He took inventory, his arm enflamed, throbbing, itching, colossally painful and tender. Otherwise he was unharmed. He could barely remember how it happened, dear Lord, make the pain stop. Other men cried out, but he bit his lip, cut it, tasted blood and realized he was thirsty. And he had to piss. Now.

"Missy. Missy, please," he croaked, unsure of his own voice.

A plump, pretty girl, a gap-toothed smile. "Yes, yes."

"Missy, I have to make water. And I am very thirsty."

"You cannot stand yet, please, let me help you. And don't worry," she smiled and reddened, "I do this all day."

Quick and efficient, she turned him to his left side, undid his buttons, and had a wood bucket in her hand. She directed him and his stream, eyes fixed. Messerel was alarmed at how fast it all happened, and looked at her shoulder, then her ear. Out of the corner of his eye he saw the same thing happening down the row of beds. His relief was overwhelming, his embarrassment gone.

It returned with the smell.

"Sorry, missy."

"That's okay. This is your bucket, if you need it. Any of us can help you, just ask. Are you in pain?" As she talked, she rubbed him down, dabbing at him, folding his garments, and pressing the bedclothes to him. Efficient, soft, quick, tender.

"Not really," he lied.

"Well, let me see if there's something we can find to help you sleep some. Please rest."

A call from across the ward, one, and then several.

"Sheila."

"Sheila."

"Sheila."

And she was gone to the next bed.

Messerel was still thirsty.

A long angled shadow came over Messerel's bed.

"What did you say to her?" Accusatory, but timid.

"What? Nothing, I said nothing. She helped me."

"I'm the guard here. Paul Musgrove. Sorry about your arm. I try to keep an eye on Sheila; soldiers might take advantage of her being nice and think it for something it isn't. She's a good girl and she should be treated right."

"Hey, uh, Musgrove, right?"

"Yeah."

"You talk too much. Can you get me some water? Then I'll listen to your bullcrap all day."

Musgrove laughed at that, spun on his crutch, and limped over to the water basin. Messerel saw the soldier was younger than he, without much of a leg, using a crutch more worn than the uniform. Didn't have a weapon with him. Not sure what Musgrove is guarding, he thought, but the girl Sheila would be worth scrapping for.

Messerel reached for the offered cup, but couldn't sit up.

"Wait. Here." Musgrove used the bed as a leg to free his hands, deftly threw an arm under Messerel, and brought the cup to the wounded man's lips. Messerel took it in one gulp.

"Thanks. More."

Musgrove was back right away. After three trips and draughts from the cup, Messerel was satisfied.

"Thanks, Musgrove."

Musgrove nodded.

"She your girl?"

"No."

"I'm Messerel. From Morristown, that's in New Jersey, with irregulars. What's today?"

"Thursday."

"Damn it, son, you can talk now. Tell me what you know."

"You've been out of it for three days. They're relieved you're awake. Your unit is long gone. You can go home as soon as you can walk."

"With Sheila and those soft hands I'll be staying awhile."

Musgrove snorted, turned on his crutch, and limped away to the main door, taking up his watch post without turning back to see Messerel, but able to keep a peripheral glance of Sheila.

If he had seen Messerel he would have witnessed the agony of a man with nowhere to go, no people to see, a man lonely and now alone, only part of what he once was. He wondered if he could stay in the army, he'd heard that cripples could still serve. . .

11

Soldiers by God

★

*A*s the days crept on the heat rose with the anxiety of engagement, then the muster of men and horses driven to a rally point to create a line, then wait then sit and then a new encampment. Prayer for another day of no shots fired, perhaps another day in place, without a futile march to nowhere but here.

Each fashioned his own crutch, or canes, or walking stick, or sling, pairing with one who compensated for his own void. The one-armed private who needed another arm, sought and found the one legged soldier who could fire a rifle but not carry it and its ammunition. These pairings were natural, made swiftly, and in the gallows humor of the first few days they called themselves the super soldier, a soldier of power, a soldier by war and forged together by God. A soldier by God.

The mustering of the 18th moved with all the grace of a herd of sheep being led by a dog that barked only at flowers. There was some shouting, more cursing, a scuffle or two, with the occasional assistance to the more infirm and less belligerent. An invalid soldier could spot the seriously wounded (and never hesitated to help), and targeted the rare malingerer. Any man missing fingers could not cry or show self-pity. A man without eyes could not judge, being completely reliant on others.

For the re-formation of the 18th that spring of 1864, two battalions were cobbled together, separated by seriousness of wounds. One eye, one hand, or an awkward healing was considered for the first battalion, while more grievous injuries, especially to the legs, were assigned to the second battalion. These criteria were not rigid, and stayed loosely defined. A soldier's conscious and unforced desire to continue to serve was paramount. Being self-ambulatory, canes and crutches for support were required. Being disease free was a conspicuously absolute condition of service in the 18th. Disease of all kinds incapacitated and killed more than hot metal. Segregation of the sick was sometimes too late to matter, and close quarters, shared supplies, and lazy habits made the situation worse tenfold. Leadership, constant and vigilant, provided the difference with soldiers cynical of death, and even the most elementary and ordinary sanitation practices were routinely flouted. Unless there was leadership.

The strength of the 18th lay in a bedrock of committed wounded. The junior leadership of the corps was woefully inadequate. Officers missing hands, an arm, an eye or even a foot were allowed to remain with their units. The officers and NCOs of the 18th were assigned, and most had terrible wounds, or were now physically ineffective in battle. There were exceptions, as in the commanding officer and his first sergeant. The drop off in effective subordinate leadership after Colonel Time and First Sergeant Kuriger was startling.

The mass of men were no more than a herd after several hours of go here, get there, baying at pain and nonsense, and a few even began to bite each other rather than throw punches. A familiar command voice, rich in hostile timber, cut through the grassy parade ground just starting to dry in the midday sun, freezing nearly a thousand wounded men in a heartbeat.

"As you were, as you were." Kuriger, hand and stump on hips, standing legs wide on a wagon used for rations, had each soldier's attention.

"Stay in position, keep a formation, columns of twos, stay seated if you must. . .and leave room for officers and physicians for an inspection of persons."

Silence. Some took the initiative to repeat the instructions by shouting down the ranks, a military echo that cascaded over several hundred wounded but able, defiant of nature but obedient to man.

Colonel Time walked down the ranks, impressed with the rough semblance of professional files of men standing, kneeling, many sitting. A physician was in tow, the only citizen soldier with all his physical faculties. His satchel was heavy with bandages. He kept pace with Time, who, with the firm gentleness of a grandparent, segregated each man to a respective battalion.

"First. Second. Second. First. Second. Third."

Time established his own criteria. The first battalion would be men able to fight. An arm missing might not disqualify if the eyes were clear, no other defects were apparent, and the soldier held Time's gaze in a challenge. The colonel respected the salty invalid, knew there was fight in a man if he kept his head up, his shoulders back. Those who sat or knelt or stared vacantly were assigned to the Second Battalion. The third was reserved for those who could not carry their own weight, and there were very few at this point. The third would be mustered out of service, with great dignity, but with speed.

Time kept few men with one foot, 'monopeds' he thought, apart from the unusually gifted or spirited, with one notable exception. The small private, Cal Straw, missing both feet, was exceedingly adept at armory repair and maintenance, small hands for small work. Most of the kept monopeds were brilliant marksmen who had an innate ability to make long-range targets very very close. A few refused to acknowledge a handicap and maintained a steely resolve that was imposing if not outright threatening. Men respect confident men. Each monoped retained stayed on his own terms, as if the decision to be a part of the Second Battalion of the Veterans' Reserve

Corps was up to himself, not an officer or doctor who could not feel his heart within.

These soldiers had all requested to remain. Not much use asking about injuries, Time mused, when the obvious would tell the tale. If the colonel had doubt as to an assignment, he did not show it.

Each invalid soldier accepted his assignment without demonstrating emotion. Time's injuries were most evident to his troops, his stature enhanced by his reputation, and a bad attitude by a soldier early in the process might get one discharged: no pay, no food, no camaraderie, no life to go to, and no purpose to live.

A soldier does what a soldier must do because of other soldiers. The flag does not drive them now, though it sometimes inspires in battle. The officers did not motivate a soldier's service, though their example compelled them forward. The idea that God created all men as equal was as alien a concept to many union soldiers as the flight of birds. The bird flew before, and always will, but that doesn't mean man could take wing and fly. Soldiers knew instinctively that there would always be inequality in the world. The hay bailer, the horseman, the farmer, craftsman, shopkeeper, lawyer, doctor, politician. . . there was a hierarchy in all of life. The soldier does not face death for equality, for the soldier could never fly.

Soldiers knew right from wrong. Owning a human was wrong.

Soldiers know injustice, and would sacrifice to defeat it.

Soldiers of the 18th, especially now, were equal.

The soldier does what the soldier must do because his brother soldier is watching him, and relying upon him. Because to fail at any task, especially in the face of danger, meant his brother may have to bear the risk he did not take. The invalid regiment was a ghostly reminder of the men they once were, when fear mixed with wonder and fate. Now they stood or knelt or carried a stool, dragged satchels, carried their brother's weapon, spat and grumbled and cried in pain with every step, for the gravest crime a soldier could commit would be to let his brother down.

The soldier does what a soldier must do for his brother to survive.

@@@

Washington, D.C., sprawled entering the summer of 1864. The rolling hills south of the Potomac in Virginia were secure from rebel incursion, and tent cities sprang up in a precise fashion pushing into Alexandria and its vicinity. A great struggle between the discipline of the army and the predictable camp followers and profiteers was the battle now fought.

The First and Second Battalions of the 18th Veterans' Reserve Corps did not have this problem. The underbelly of normalcy surrounding armies at war, the prostitute, the card player, the moonshine salesman, all avoided the invalids. The soldiers were social pariahs, though not low denizens of it. A few brave women, women of nursing skill, were trusted and honored by the 18th. No others.

The Veterans' Reserve Corps would take care of its own.

The First Battalion was formed with six companies of eighty men each. Their training was uninterrupted by the military penchant for administration, though all levels of leadership were determined, transferring their stoicism to each battle hardened and broken soldier. The First was planned to train like a complete fighting unit, separate from the Second Battalion. After Time's initial muster of his regiment of the corps, the two battalions made infrequent planned contact.

The Second Battalion also started with six companies of five hundred total men. Their mission was simple but crucial. The Second would provide guard duty for supplies, for bounty men, and for prisoners. Any soldier who could not stand for duty could sit. The men of the Second displayed a cooperative nature not common for an army at war. Assignments were given and then bartered, and for the first few weeks there were no disciplinary problems while in garrison, also unusual for soldiers. Garrison duty was boring, repetitive, and sometimes without purpose except to stay busy. The men of the Second embraced being busy, useful, and consequential. Duty shifts were shortened to accommodate demand for work. Every soldier had a hand in the unit's purpose, and each man relied on this esprit to carry himself through his own pain of heart and limb.

The First Battalion was gradually stripped because of front line attrition and need, the vast majority moving to regiments closer to the enemy and performing rear guard duties, meshing seamlessly with their brothers in the field. Some drifted to the Second. Some of the Second were discharged by necessity.

The Second Battalion stayed together, as outcast as a leper colony. Time remained with the Second. Kuriger remained with Time.

At the indefinable moment when garrison monotony threatened to become boredom the Second was ordered to move. The only thing soldiers crave more than routine is forward motion. The logistical detail of assembling, rationing and outfitting the nearly five hundred men of the Second Battalion created a feverish inertia of activity that affected the men to greater reserves of strength, both physical and emotional. Hospital lay-abouts and pitiable wretches, no more. The men of the Second Battalion were on the move.

@@@

Orders were made, written, read, given, and reviewed. The Second Battalion would take several boats and drift down the Potomac to Belle Plain, overnight, less than 40 miles south of Washington. A sturdy skiff was acquired for the transportation of nurses. The men smiled and joked that forced marches were now for the other poor damn bastards.

A late spring squall made for sloppy embarkation, and the initial zeal became haste and all the attendant miscues and irretrievable waste of supplies, most notably tents. Stores of foodstuffs, small arms and ammunition, powder, boots, uniforms and medical supplies were placed in a single low draft schooner with short sails, the *Gibraltar*. The men were split up in companies between another eight boats of dubious safety and not intended to transport masses of men, especially wounded and the near crippled. The rain would not let up. Wind was not important, as the Potomac would move any boat, with or without sail. The most acute problem was that beyond a screaming deck hand or two, the soldiers were no more than passengers, observed and observant, but without any utility. The few who managed to offer help to hold this line, pull that line, secure that hatch or boom or sail cursed their own stupidity. The squalls grew worse, Belle Plain beckoned, and a portion of the Second Battalion on the *Gibraltar* took cover from the driving cold rain below decks.

The stench there was rancid and thick, coming in slow pushes like the slap of the wakes that incessantly swelled against the sides of the boat. A platoon of Lieutenant William Tecumseh Anderson's company was crowded on the *Gibraltar* and sat shoulder to shoulder, chest to knee to stump, directly on crates or torn gunwales. Some wood was rotting. Indirect light seeped in before the dusk but was accompanied by buckets of rain. Cautious of each other's infirmities, the soldiers avoided talking as the odor was too overwhelming and opening one's mouth would carry the taste of filth for long minutes. A rumor ran through the darkness of the hold, to urinate on a handkerchief and hold it to your nose to quiet the smell. No one tried it, but the thought of it kept their humor light, which started a round of comically unnecessary questions:

"Do you have a silk handkerchief I could borrow?"

"I haven't blown my nose with one hand yet."

"Hold this while I piss on it."

"Why not crap in your hat?"

"I did, why do you think it smells so hell-awful."

The small things were always returning as big things. Clearing one's nose was an indelicate exercise under the best conditions, but made easy if just a matter of plugging one hole and snorting out the other. Buckling belts. Buttoning trousers and blouses. The soldier who had two boots to tie invariably had only one hand to tie them, and no matter how dexterous it was never quite right. The man with one hand was fascinated at the action of his remaining lifeline to a productive life, flexing his fingers, keeping it in view, thinking it too might vanish in a spray of blood or be cut off in his dreams.

Lieutenant Anderson had the same dream every night, and the prospect of getting on the *Gibraltar* with his company frightened him. In his dreams, for months now, even before he lost his hand, *he was adrift in an endless pool of undulating water, speckled with hard rain, sky a slack grey without a shoreline in sight. He knew it was a dream even as he slept, but the water carried him up and down, swirled about him, and became heavy and cold. Waves would tower above him, rush to his head, and then carry him skyward, still a deep grey pitch. His arms could not move, the end of his right arm a balloon where his hand belonged. He could swim, but he didn't need to. Calling out was futile. The only things that changed in the dream were those with him; his father was there many times, his sisters in turn less so. Schoolmates and town characters from Four Mile all showed up briefly, but most often now fellow officers and men of units past and present. Everyone asked him the same thing: "What will you do?"*

And Will never answered, too busy keeping his head up, too busy being frightened. He could not force himself to sleep, and always succumbed to exhaustion, his father's words in his dreams.

"Stand your ground in the face of evil, Will, and you shall never kneel to fear."

The embarkation of the *Gibraltar* caused him much anxiety, more than other troop movements. He saw the churning Potomac and the incessant driving rain and the hair on the back of his calves rose and pricked like a thousand needles. His men now grumbled that they were not riding in paddle wheel ferries that able soldiers had available to them, and he had no answer, no retort to the false claim. He could only stare at the water and the hastening darkness of twilight.

A call went out that the boats could begin pushing off when ready. It was to be a steady float, reaching the shores of Belle Plain before dawn.

The hold of the *Gibraltar* was flat-bottomed and sturdy, but dank and fetid. The men sat tight against each other, shoulder to shoulder, and as human cargo knew that a cooperative and light hearted attitude would work wonders and make the transport go smoothly.

Until the puking started. The soldiers of the 18th had endured much in the months of the war, and would endure more as the years of their lives not yet perceived wore on, plodded, and were envisioned in their darkest moments. Some would not survive the war, and others would not survive the peace when it came. Some of them believed that life could not get worse, though most of them knew they had been blessed with consciousness and spirit. All of them thought a boat ride might be something of a treat.

Until the puking started.

And it didn't take long.

No one was certain who vomited first, but events happened too quickly to assess blame or offer recriminations. Only Perks was exempt, as he stated at least a dozen times that he hadn't eaten anything for hours, skipping evening chow before the embarkation. He had tried to go above decks, but the wind and squalling rain were difficult, and the civilian sailors shouted him and intrepid others back into the hold. Human cargo, covered in puke.

One soldier puked in his hat, and another followed suit, and then a speedy domino of successive heaves that startled everyone in ferocity and pungency. In minutes half the soldiers aboard had expended themselves and were gagging in dry heaves like so many baying mules.

Perks laughed, long and hard. This, too, proved just as infectious, the absurdity of sitting with a campaign hat full of puke with nowhere to go gnawing at each man in turn. The booming guffaw of Thunder, not heard in months by any nor by most of the unit ever at all, sent even the sickest soldiers into breathless spasms of laughter, and a few soldiers now openly mocked the vomiting ones, feigning an upset constitution. This was rewarded by thrown puke, more riotous yelling, some rough shoving and one ear tip bitten clean off. This act seemingly sent the ship rocking harder in gales of hysterics, as the surf buffeted the *Gibraltar*, and the rain drummed above, and eventually the soldiers of the 18th gave in to exhaustion and fell into a rank and restless slumber.

The boats in the flotilla arrived well before dawn, and the word was passed that the men could not disembark until accommodation for weapons and gear was made. This was fully and immediately ignored, as the men of each and every boat in the flotilla were in no better shape than the *Gibraltar*'s cargo, and in the hour before dawn the entire battalion washed themselves, their uniforms, and each other in the cold embrace of the late spring Potomac.

@@@

Unlikely pairs happened without rancor, like Musgrove and Messerel, who attached to each other naturally. Most men could not stand next to the boorish, or the cowardly, or the indecisive, or the inflexible, or the unfocused, or the unprofessional, or the undisciplined, or the uptight, or the loud, the confused, the troublesome, the atheist, the deist; none of that now.

George Huntred was drafted for the duty of carrying Cal Straw by the colonel himself. Time took a shine to the young legless soldier, whom the entire regiment could see, but by which the colonel knew he had to find a suitable job, not letting Cal ride the supply wagon, nor have Thunder pull it like a horse. He would not let Huntred be a beast of burden.

These two have spirit, Time thought, I should send them home, but. . .

The sadness of the giant Thunder was evident to all, and the alertness of the young private Straw had improved Thunder's morale. Cal weighed little more than a full sack of grain, much less than two. To Thunder, he was light, easily maneuverable, and was his eyes. Suitable work for a soldier of the 18th.

"Just walk, George, I'll keep us out of gopher holes."

It took less than a hundred yards of walking around the garrisoned tents in the shadow of Washington for George and Cal to develop a system of nudges, shifts, and short commands. Cal was sensitive but amusing to George. The trust was quickly absolute. By their arrival in Belle Plain they moved as one, silently.

There was a pretense of rigid military order that was to be maintained, mostly in respect to routine garrison demands. Reveille, guard posting and hours, chow, latrine order, the chain of command were kept. Fueling courage and the necessity of drill to occupy a dull existence were history. Most had proved their courage just by volunteering, even if the wound was from hiding from the ferocity of battle. The only drill was live or dry fire exercise by sitting, kneeling, standing or prone. Missing a hand did not deter a committed marksman, but did make reloading time-consuming. If the soldier had an elbow, his dexterity was acquired through practice. Missing an eye made rifle work difficult but not impossible, but close work, like re-loading, could be performed with skill after practice. There was an intense unspoken commitment to be fast and sure and useful, to remain consequential, so that the smallest of tasks were worked with the greatest of focus.

The larger world, the war, was small and secondary to these men. The ability to unbutton trousers without assistance or lace a boot with one hand was the difference between degradation and dignity. Small things were very big indeed.

Men talked, especially in pairs. The men of the 18th had an esprit, a confidence in themselves amongst themselves, which did not exist when their shell was whole, in the life before. The average soldier told tall tales, laughed at everything ugly and absurd, and spoke with a courage untested, but the men of the 18th had a grander humor, and spoke little in large groups, averted eyes when focused on their own limitation, and guarded their pair partner's safety like a loyal hound.

Men can be comfortable in silence, too, especially in pairs. Soldiers doubly so. The veterans of the 18th lapsed into silence instead of speaking, quietly assisting or gesturing with limbs, shoulder, and head. The profundity of the spoken word was reserved for only the truly remarkable. Calling attention to the humorous and absurd, or an alarm, or a philosophical entreaty, and then the words were spoken with authority in a measured and hushed tone.

Talk of the life left behind was limited. Most of the men of the 18th had not been seen by kin, and were still ruminating about the inevitable reception. Many had stopped writing letters, and a few had never told the folks back home anything except that they were wounded but still serving, very busy, much safer now, pray for me, I think of you in my dreams, God Bless.

In quieter moments, off guard, the soldiers of the Veterans' Corps talked of God, and how and why He could see this destruction and death and disfigurement and do anything but weep for humanity.

"The Lord's wrath is why this never ends," whispered George, as he sat next to Cal.

"George, you should sleep. You carried me all day. You make me tired thinking about it," Cal stretched his slight frame, hands behind his head, looking at the cloudless night sky filled with stars.

George was undeterred. "God doesn't want us to war, so our punishment is it never ending. Or our blindness or cut off arms and legs."

He said this flatly, without venom or anger, as if talking to himself. George did not like sleep, and hadn't slept properly since the explosion. Though blind, when awake he was connected to what was around him. When he slept, *the demon came to him, crawling out of the earth, silent but vivid, angry, bringing bile to George's tongue. He would try to cough, not certain if he was awake or asleep, the demon receding into the earth, now crawling out again, much closer, watching George, changing shape into a wolf, teeth bared, eyes red and glowing with hate. The demon always came to George before sleep took him completely away, and only when exhaustion overwhelmed him did George find a rest like death. The slightest noise, or rolling onto a small rock, or an insect alighting on his head would wake him, and the cycle of the demon wolf crawling out of the earth, closer, evil in intent, would start again.*

"George." Cal sensed the giant's restlessness and misery.

"Yes."

"George, without you, I would be dead now, many times, I think. God brought you to the 18ᵗʰ and made us partners. Praise Him, George. God has given you someone to carry in the darkness."

"Cal, you funny. God gave me you, to see for me, right? I don't think I could carry Old Irish. He sounds like a load."

They both laughed silently.

"Cal."

"Yes."

"I don't much like to sleep anymore."

@@@

12

Evil

*T*he farmhouses in the vicinity of Belle Plain were functional, unadorned, and fiercely held for the first years of the war by proud Virginians. As the Union Army descended southward in the winter, spring and summer of 1864, territory became plunder, and what was not destroyed by retreating landowners was commandeered for use by the advancing army of northern aggression. No landowners in northern Virginia held large untouched estates. Most were slave-less homesteaders now, and their resentment and bitterness toward both armies and the war in general was intense. If they stayed, it was to protect their property. The displaced watched the union soldiers with a radiant hatred, and the union soldiers eyed the homesteaders with foul humor and high suspicion.

Homes became quarters for officers or wounded, sometimes both, so some care was taken to keep the premises neat and orderly, though not altogether clean. Churches were not exempt from the need to house wounded and perform hospital services. One smallish church in ill-repair would be chosen for hospital work over a new and freshly painted house of worship. The taller the church, the less likely it would be utilized by the army for the sick and dying. Those wounded men who could walk out of a hospital often did, sometimes back to a unit, sometimes on a long and arduous walk home. It was too much work to police a hospital, most often staffed with a doctor or veterinarian and several women who came with the land. These particular women-made-nurses, initially horror stricken with the overwhelming sights and stench of death, with husbands and brothers and sons and beaus either off to war or already dead themselves, had had enough of sitting and waiting.

A church on the eastern side of Belle Plain adjacent to a self sustaining homestead was ideal for a regiment on the mend, too far south to return to Washington, though too wounded and decimated to move farther in support of Grant. The home was a one-story, ideal for a headquarters, with a separate shack for food preparation. The church, a chapel, was away from the road, behind a copse of trees, nearly forgotten, abandoned as a parish by default, and without a preacher. It was old, but well constructed. The inside eaves were not large, and the bench pews were forced together to make bed frames, about twenty in all. Each makeshift hospital bed was occupied. The long sides of the chapel had abundant windows, low sills, and most were intact. Its location was ideal, a peculiarity of terrain and tree growth. Wind in winter would not flow here, but in the summer months the rush of wind from the Potomac through the shaded trees was cooling.

Four women hustled from bed to bed with water or bandages or nourishment or a tender hand. Two were matronly, two were young, and all were related in some way to each other, or Belle Plain, or had travelled south with the 18th. As the sun lowered activity slowed, and except for an occasional call from a wounded soldier, there was little to do this evening. The doctor would not be coming until morning.

The infirmary was an oasis of pain. To be in garrison, drilling, was monotony. To be on the march, building fence barricades or digging trenches was brutal drudgery, but purposeful if gains were made, or the rations improved. To be in the assault was hair-raising, fire-breathing, shaken and fierce, awful in blood, exhilarating in the fight, the kill. And then death brought peace.

Garrison, the march, and the assault were all better than the infirmary, which was as much death's antechamber as poor field position or confused leadership. The infirmary was a disharmony of moans and prayers, as sharp and predictable as cicadas on hot summer nights. To the grievously wounded, the infirmary was a parlor of the devil's home, where you waited before being shown into the dining room of the beast. The infirmary, to one of sound mind, was hell.

One of the two young girls was moving hurriedly between all the beds, tending quickly and efficiently to the wounded. She had a shallow pan with clean water, many dry rags over her shoulder, and a moist cotton rag in the basin that was soft to the touch, absorbent, and functional. She moved to a bed, whispered, "Bath for you, quickly, sir," and gently washed what was needed. The girl rinsed the cotton rag, took a dry one from her shoulder, and dried the moist areas, folded whatever uniform blouse there was over the wounded, and then moved on. For every three soldiers, she used the same water, and then darted outside to toss the pan's grey contents, get more water from the well, and start anew.

The quiet nobleness of nursing will humble the most injured of men.

The soldier's memory of battle was never more acute than when present here. Some saw their wounds with indifference, vowing to be the one man who lived, fought, survived, and overcame. But the cold reality of living without what others took for granted came crashing down every dawn, and haunted the last glimpse of consciousness before the release of sleep every night.

The racks were organized by type of injury. The women kept faithful records, took pride in it, and were convinced their ministrations were enhanced by a military precision of created paperwork. All but six men were amputees. Four of these had severe head wounds, were breathing, but were largely unresponsive. Of the remaining two, one was blinded and the other catatonic, eyes wide, mumbling "rocks and grass" over and over, clenching and unclenching his fists, occasionally squeezing his eyes shut and gargling. One of the young nurses thought it was all a charade, but that was dispelled after nearly thirty hours of constant and unerring repetition.

"Ma'am, may I go now? I cannot stand any longer," the one girl bathing the men said to her matron, pleadingly.

"Of course, dear. Both of you young ladies may go. Run along, straight to the house, before it gets dark."

The girls needed no further encouragement, bolting for the double doors, brushing past a large figure in the doorway.

He stood unsteadily, shifting from foot to foot, not in a uniform of any kind. His long coat was torn, hat over his eyes, and a bandana was secured over his nose, hiding the lower half of his face. With the setting sun illuminating behind him, his visage was frightening for what could not be seen.

The matron thought him a bandit. The other woman clung to her.

"You'll find no money here, or food. This is a hospital."

He raised his head, his eyes imploring, whites wide, black at the center. Tears welled.

"I know, ma'am." A nasty phlegmy lisp. "I have a face wound, my jaw. I am an old conscript with a new unit. I need a bandage and soap, please."

He looks sincere, she thought. He sounds worse.

"I will take a look at you."

"No."

"But I can help. Are you bleeding?"

"No. But it weeps. I can manage on my own. Please."

The women looked at each other.

"I have left my rifle there." He pointed to the door-jamb. "I just need to clean my wound, bandage again, and sit a spell, away from all. . . of this." His chest heaved and their hearts would have broken then, but they had been hardened by the effect and refuse of war, wounded men.

"Very well. Stay here for an hour, will you? We need to walk about before it gets too cold and too dark. We expect a sentry to be by before eight o'clock." It was not yet seven now.

"Thank you, ma'am. Good night."

He touched his hat brim. The women left.

The man closed the door behind them. He could not believe his good fortune. He smiled, and started to slide the bandana down. He stopped, as he could not risk being recognized. It was not from a wound of war that he hid his face, but one possessed from birth. He had scouted the matrons' habits, and knew their pattern. Tonight that pattern would be exploited.

He walked slowly down the center of the infirmary, looking intently left, then right, then back again, in rhythm with his gait. He was looking for something. Prey. A weakness. The man made no sound, as his deed would not be one that welcomed witnesses. He grabbed several scraps of cloth bandages, thrusting them into his coat pocket without missing a step.

The predator drifted toward the left, and the second farthest rack next to a window. In the fading glow of the sunset the view outside the open frame was almost idyllic. A lilac bush was shedding its blooms, yet it stood regally a few feet away, and then dense brush behind it, then the trees. A good escape route, he thought. I shall not leave from the front. The stolen rifle might be discovered as missing soon enough, and an alarm would be raised. It being at this infirmary could be explained.

There. A young soldier. Severely bandaged, already lying on his side, facing away from his approach. He didn't appear to be breathing; just as well, he thought. I'll make this quick.

@@@

Henry Parker and his eight-year-old son, Henry, were poised in the thicket of trees outside the last window of the chapel, farthest from the doors. Henry wasn't sure if there was food there, or blankets, or any comforts. He knew he and his son must stay hidden until it was fully dark. They watched two girls leave, followed a few minutes later by two older women. I think it's empty, Henry thought, but I cannot be certain. His eyes were failing him even though he was not yet thirty. He had to get closer.

"Henry stay here. I'm going to the window to look in."

"Yes, Daddy, yes. But, but wait. I see someone walking in there," just as soft, into his father's ear.

Fully alert now, eyes wide, Henry realized his night vision was worse than ever. He could barely see the outline of the window, and certainly nothing beyond it. The window was open, enough for a man to crawl through. Young Henry would have to make the entry, grab whatever he could, praise the Lord, and then back to Mary and his daughter.

"Henry," whispered his father, "I can't see that clearly. You get close to the window, and peek in, and find a couple blankets, food, too, and push them out the window. I'll grab them, pull you out, and we go back to our little camp. You remember how to get there?"

"Yes, Daddy. But there's a man right there, at the window. Right there."

"Does he see us?"

"I don't think so, Daddy. But it looks like he's tending to a soldier."

"Stay still. Wait."

Henry's vision adjusted, and he now saw the man moving in the window. He saw the head clearly, but could not see the face from the mask. Henry thought the man might be scratching himself, his crotch, and knew there was something wrong, a perversion about him. He hoped his son would not understand, seeing this drifter and his bizarre ritual.

The man inside removed his handkerchief from his face, and both Henrys gasped. The man looked up at the sound from outside.

What was that? The man thought, was it outside or in here? He whipped his head around once, twice, and there was no movement from within the infirmary. Have I imagined it? Sounded like a cough. The handkerchief floated to the ground.

He stared out the window for many long seconds, seeing nothing. The lilac bush had blended into the brush and tree line in the enveloping darkness. He held his stare, and sucked at his only tooth, a large canine offset from his face but seated under a harelip that reached his left nostril. Fate placed a strong sharp tooth at the only place where he would have regretted it, and the effect of the ruptured lip, scattered whiskers and single sharp tooth was monstrous.

He was called Dogtooth. He had been humiliated by what fate handed him all his life, abandoned by all, and had become a hard-hearted cold animal proud of the fear he instilled in others. His malevolence oozed like the mucous he was constantly snorting or spitting or swallowing. He ran his tongue, serpentine, around the large canine tooth, and smiled. He enjoyed his practices, even the small ones.

The interruption broke his concentration, but not his intent. His privates were exposed, prepared for sodomy, and he started to act quickly, heedless of any potential threat. He pulled the sheet back off the soldier he had chosen for his rape and was surprised the young man's buttocks were exposed. He sucked hard at his single tooth and reached to stroke the wounded man, touched him, and suddenly drew back.

This soldier must be dead, he thought. He's cold. What little light the room held in the glow of oil lamps confirmed it. The soldier was ashen-blue.

Then there'll be no fight in him, Dogtooth snorted to himself. Best get right to it. . .

"*STOP.*"

Henry Parker threw up the window, and attempted to jump the sill in one bound, with both hands, but fell away to the ground onto his back. Young Henry yelped.

Trousers at his knees, Dogtooth stumbled back and suppressed a shout. Where did that Negro come from, he thought. The infirmary began to stir like a wave of consciousness, and he knew that recognition must be avoided. He had only one option, and with his trousers pulled up and half secured, he jumped out the window just as Henry Parker was making his second attempt to enter it.

Both men locked in mid-air, but Dogtooth had the leverage, and they fell, hard, onto the ground below. Young Henry kicked the ugly man in the back once, twice, and then both men disengaged. Each had more to lose by being caught by authorities than they did in winning a fist fight.

"You are worse than an animal."

"Runaway, now, isn't you." Dogtooth reached for the boy.

"I'll kill you first," growled Henry, driving both hands into the face and chest of the man, throwing him backwards.

"Who goes there?" A sentry called from the front of the building, alerted by the muffled sounds of the struggle.

Henry Parker let go of Dogtooth and dove for the darkness at the building's corner. Dogtooth sprinted into the woods, and young Henry vaulted himself into the infirmary through the open window, landing lightly.

Young Henry heard no other sounds. His eyes adjusted immediately to the weak light of the infirmary lanterns. He saw the dead half-naked soldier to his left, and quickly covered the man's lower torso. He knew blankets were needed, and another night without them would have been unbearable. He would find a blanket for his mother. Move quietly.

Henry, prone and immobile, heard footsteps approach, light and tentative. He was enveloped in the dark, the tree line was close, and discovery would have been fatal. He would not leave without his son. He did not know if the interloper to the fight was a soldier or a passer-by. But he knew he might be armed.

The steps slowed as they drew nearer. Henry would not dare to lift his head. He had fallen awkwardly, fully out of sight from the side of the chapel. The sentry or whoever would have to step into the pitch darkness behind the building, and then step on Henry in order to see him. Stay still. Boy, he thought, stay still. Henry had seen his son vault and dive up and into the open window, without a sound. He prayed quickly that the sentry had not seen the boy in the confusion, and had focused on Dogtooth's noisy exit into the dense tree line.

The steps stopped. A minute passed. The sentry har-rumphed and began walking away at a steady pace. Henry Parker could feel the relief of him departing. He ventured a look, over his shoulder, and saw the sentry turn the corner at the head of the chapel, and heard him mount steps. He'll find the boy soon enough, he knew. Got to move.

Henry sprang to his haunches and tip toed to the window.

"Henry."

"Daddy."

"Let's go."

Young Henry handed his father two wool blankets and several bed sheets. Henry lifted his son through the window, set him down, and they took off into the woods.

Damned if that animal he fought with wasn't heading in the direction of Mary and the baby, Henry thought. The brush has been bent and is giving us a path to follow.

"C'mon, son. We have to hurry. Can you take the sheets?"

"I'll carry them all, Daddy. I know where Momma is."

"Good. Good boy. I have to hurry." Henry started to sprint to where his wife and baby girl were hiding.

@@@

Mary Parker and little May sat still in the quickening darkness, enveloped in the silence of twilight, listening to the awakening of all God's night creatures. They were hungry. Mary knew that she and her two-year-old would be cold soon, again. They could be patient, as they had been for the past ten days. But they must be quiet.

The Parkers had left a small plantation in North Carolina in the dead of night, with only the clothes on their backs. Henry had worked plowing and tilling, from sunrise to sunset all his life. Mary worked the field, too, but instead of brute power she was constantly bending, weeding, and moving rock. At a glance the work seemed less arduous than plowing, but the constant up down bend grip walk up down bend grip was back breaking and mind numbing.

They had decided to leave after the second miscarriage. The work was too strenuous, the shack they lived in was too worn, and their food was becoming less and less balanced, tasteless and increasingly sparse. The owner and overseer were both off to war, and the operation was being run by the absent boss's dullish brother, Junior. He was threatening more than a lash, and the Parkers knew that it was only a matter of time before the strain of the small plantation's failure would cause a catastrophe. Junior was a bomb looking for a spark. The effect of it all on young Henry was the pity of it. He had to dodge Junior's anger at every turn. Young Henry, who they called Henry Two, was bright, open, and eager to please. But the scars and broken bones that came with a lash or a cane would beat goodness right out of him. It was their great fear.

Henry and Mary had no ill will toward the owner himself, but in his absence under Junior's hand the plantation was close to ruin. They still distrusted the owner, for the most part, and all white people absolutely.

Henry and Mary had seen too much devastation of other slaves, and the deteriorating arc of the quality of life during the war years opened their eyes to the possibility of flight. They kept close their counsel. After the last miscarriage, Henry said they would all leave as soon as Mary was ready.

A fortnight later they slipped out just after sunset.

They dead reckoned north. Staying close to the road, but never on it, Henry had a loose sense of direction from the sun, but all their movement would have to be at night. It was very slow going, and their only real safety would be in distance and speed.

They had not gone far enough. The terrain worked against them. Most of the daylight hours were devoted to sleep in hiding, and night travel was slow. More than once they had stumbled badly, Henry carrying both children, a cry would go out, and they'd stop and wait, resuming a steady march if no retort.

Mary smelled something burning through the trees. She knew that she and the baby would need to stay put, but the flames beckoned, the promise of warmth and perhaps food. The scent of roasting meat came to her, and May, too. Both stomachs rumbled. The child grew restless and fidgety. Mary would have tried to give her daughter her own milk, but she had stopped producing yesterday. She was starving, and now her baby would, also.

They stared at the flickering flame through the trees, thoughts darting between food and praying that Henry and the boy would return soon. They had been gone for what seemed like hours.

May started to cry, and Mary held her tightly, cooing to her, fairly begging her to be soothed. The light and darkness were playing tricks, and for a moment Mary thought she had dozed off, with the child still inconsolable.

The flames through the trees grew faint, and then she felt a man standing over her. Not her man.

Mary looked up into a white face with a wild shock of light greasy hair. The beard was curiously well-kept, in stark contrast to the disheveled clothes and odor coming from him. He held a cudgel in his hand. He leaned close to Mary's face, and the child grew silent. Mary saw that his beard was bright red, and his eyes were deep black.

"Runaway, yes. You would fetch a good reward if I wasn't already wanted by the law."

And he raised the cudgel over his shoulder, coming down once, twice; then once more.

@@@

Dogtooth tore through the woods, knowing the terrain, sure-footed but panicked. The slave was behind him, not on his heels, but too close for him to slow down. The child, if he still was with him, would prevent the slave from overtaking him soon. That one had real menace in his eyes. The runaway said he'd kill him, and he meant it. Dogtooth knew a bluff, and that wasn't it.

The Negro might not catch him, but he could track him. Dogtooth was creating distance, but not enough to lose the angered slave and boy. Why wouldn't he run away from me, he thought, he can get away clean without a tussle with me. Dogtooth wanted desperately to avoid an unarmed fight with this Negro, who had hands of stone and a barrel chest and Dogtooth knew he would not survive the next confrontation.

Fear propelled Dogtooth, but exhaustion was taking its toll. The slave was still behind him; he could hear the boy's occasional yelp, but could not see through the dense foliage in the night. Dogtooth thought he knew how a deer must feel, sure of its footing, but frightened to keep moving forward.

Dogtooth sensed the camp was nearby, but there was no fire. Once he found the fire, and Redbeard, the slave would be only a problem, not a disaster.

He was close. There was a gully up ahead that served as a latrine on occasion, for soldiers or passer-by, and he needed to skirt it to get to a rise and then two quick short ridges and the fire would be there. Why couldn't he see it yet?

He cut hard before the gully, and nearly collided with Redbeard, who was breathing heavily from exertion. The gully was holding stagnant water, and grease and muck made for a foul odor. In the dim of the evening light, the reflected surface was broken by rock and timber, and a large dark form.

"There's a slave behind me. Chasing me. He caught me at the hospital. Why he's following me I. . ."

"Quiet, fool," growled Redbeard. He knew the slave would be coming this way.

"Hey, he's strong, and said he'd kill me and he means it."

"Quiet," lower, intent, listening. "Stay here, low. Do nothing."

Redbeard took two steps and crouched low by a tree just before the ground dropped off. He could see the frame of the Negro stop where the woman and child had been hiding. The slave whipped his head back and forth, and charged directly toward where Redbeard was hiding. As Henry Parker began to pick up his pace, running into the gully, Redbeard struck at his right knee viciously with the cudgel. Henry howled and fell like a stone. Redbeard kicked Henry Parker in the face once, disengaged the weapon buried in Henry's leg, and drove it in one clean swoop into the side of his skull.

Silence.

"Get out here, Dog."

"Why did that fool keep chasing me?"

"Come here. Grab his legs."

The men picked the body up at both ends, and walked the few yards to the gully, and with a one, two, and three, threw the body into the pool with a strangled splash.

"Make sure he sinks."

Dogtooth stepped gingerly down the short slope to where a path was beaten, and saw that the slave was face down, but on the surface, not underneath. He cursed what he had to do, not for humanity, but for the filth and grease he would trample in. He stepped into the shallow latrine and his foot struck something not rock or timber or brush, but yielding.

The bodies of Mary and May were already partially submerged, held down by rocks and forest debris. Dogtooth groaned, looked about and called out to Redbeard.

"I'll need a few large stones."

"There are some over here. Say, did this slave have a dog?"

Dogtooth hesitated, faking a groan. If I tell him about the boy, we'll be out here all night looking for him. Or he'll kill me in a rage.

"What? A dog? No, why?"

"Quiet." They stood silent for several minutes, and then both men started kicking the ground looking for large stones to weigh down the body of Henry Parker.

@@@

Young Henry stayed silent. He could clearly see the outline of that ugly man and the larger man, the one with the hammer. Wedged between a standing tree and a fallen one, Henry could only sit and wait for those men to leave. I hope Momma is hiding, thought Henry Two. I have to take care of her now.

@@@

George and Cal were absent without permission, technically deserters, having come to this place after leaving the makeshift infirmary in fear and disgust. It was night.

The boat ride, though absurdly amusing, did not help their despair. Cal's legs had healed as best as expected, but the memory of wailing and moaning in the hospital ward was more than he could bear. Both he and Thunder had been in the sickest of sick wards, and even though the food and care and cleanliness were very good, the dispirit of pain and suffering was maddening.

"Thank you for doing this, George."

The giant laughed softly. "Thanks for making sure we don't walk off a cliff."

Cal was perched across the shoulders of George, like a prized deer kill. After a few rough minutes of adjustment, Cal hooked his hip into the back of George's neck, leg stumps scissored over George's left shoulder, and his left hand gripped the front of the giant's tunic. His right cradled their water and two makeshift bedrolls. George's rifle was slung barrel down over the front of his chest. If attacked, Cal thought, we're dead. If I can get a marauder close to George he can strangle him. But in a gunfight, we're dead.

"George, you're doing great."

"Thanks, Cal. I wanna step it out a little."

George walked surely but slowly, preferring a secure foot strike to a broken ankle. The soldiers had developed a rhythm and code for obstacles, with Cal tugging George's tunic left or right, fore and aft, to keep George moving unimpeded. Most of their communication was silent, with an occasional yelp by Cal warning of a hole or such detected too late for being non-verbal, and both men knew that the night would only protect them if they were quiet. George was somewhat sensitive to sound and smell, mostly because he needed to rely on them and Cal's judgment. His blindness was total.

"I'm tired, Cal. Let's rest."

"Yeah. We can stay here for the night. I don't hear any water, but we'll find more at light."

George stooped and set Cal down and knelt. Cal took the blankets, shook them, and set them out. He reflected to himself that they would have to go back to the 18ᵗʰ at Belle Plain. At the Second, they could make themselves useful. The unplanned walk alone with George gave him confidence they could contribute. Desertion was not the answer.

"Here, George, this is your rack."

Thunder felt then spread out on the folded blanket, sighed, and would have drifted quickly to sleep, almost.

"Water, George?"

"No." And he slept, the demon dream not yet begun.

Cal had a problem. He had to make a call of nature, and he was skittish about where to go. He could see some reflected starlight through the trees and brush, and he took in the thicket of the wood he found himself in. He was painfully realizing they could not get far on their own. He did not want to go back to an infirmary. George was of a same mind. Yet both of them knew their helplessness was final, permanent, and futile to ignore. They had to return to the Second Battalion, at first light.

But at this moment he had to go, and fast. George snored. Cal pushed himself, backward, by his hands, looking over his shoulder every second push. He smelled what he thought might be a latrine, assuming it was either that or a dead animal. Yes, he thought, a privy. One more push.

The ground wasn't there where he pressed his right hand, and in an effort to recover, he lost the grip on his left; he hit his back and slid a few feet, now falling, the smell stronger than ever.

Dear God, he thought in horror, I'm going headfirst into a latrine.

He felt the grip of a small but strong hand on his left wrist, and his momentum stopped abruptly. Cal thought it was the talons of a predator bird at first.

"What. . ."

"I got you," said Henry Two, barely above a whisper. "But I can't hold you long."

Cal's eyes oriented and adjusted, but not his body. A small Negro boy had his wrist in an iron grip, and was himself holding a root from a larger tree with his other hand, with the same intensity and concentrated power.

"You hold tight, my arms is working fine." Cal moved his right arm in an arc and gripped the boy's shirt, which started to give way. He dug his fingers into the boy's shoulder, the one holding the anchor root, and yet the child didn't flinch.

"Sorry, I'll climb over you."

Hand over hand Cal reached the root, and gripped the boy in a hug, securing them both.

"George," hollered Cal, "Come help us."

"Cal, keep talking." George crawled in their direction, Cal talking him to them.

"I'm gonna hand you a small boy. He saved my life, George, he was just here and I fell and there you have him."

George grabbed the boy. "Climb on my back and hold on."

He did. "Don't choke me," growled Thunder.

"Reach out, George, and I'll be in your hand."

George pulled. The three scrambled away, all pushing with their hands, scraping their tails on the ground. They reached the blankets.

"I still have to go, George, right now."

"Come with me," said the boy, "Can you. . ."

"Yes, I can scoot fairly well, but I don't want to go near that drop again, into that privy."

"That's a grave, mister." Henry's eyes were hollow, downcast. "You come with me."

"Not far," said George, knowing that he was not of much help, but relieved they now had a guide, of sorts.

The dark and rot and undergrowth and stench would not leave them soon. After several long yards, Cal decided he could do his business right there.

"This'll do. Don't go anywhere," he whispered.

Young Henry Parker sat and looked away. He heard the soldier with no legs struggle briefly with his britches, and wondered why they moved away from the giant soldier. His hunger was acute. Two days, and this the third night. He had tried, agonizingly, to reach his father, mother, and sister in the stagnant pool. He knew they were dead, beyond hope. They were face down, mostly submerged in the muck. As the sun died each day the bodies grew, but sank, equally slowly, without urgency. Flies and beetles came and went. Even the animals of the wood avoided this spot. Henry ate leaves, lapped dew, and walked in circles. He cried, he prayed, he begged his Daddy to get up. He sang sweetly, softly. He thought he saw his mother move every now and then. He slept. When he awoke, he thought himself dreaming but the rank odor tore him back to the reality and the agony. Everyone he loved was dead. And he had no idea what to do next.

His Daddy had risked the life of his family to stop a man from. . . what?

Henry heard the rustle of the legless soldier, who was about the same size as himself. He turned, and faced the soldier, and started to ask. . .

"Come closer," Cal whispered, gesturing.

Henry did, but not too close. He had seen too many white people turn nasty even after the greatest of kindnesses of black folk. Saving the legless soldier from certain drowning in the stagnant muck would not prevent an indignity.

"What's you name?" A light, friendly whisper.

"Henry. Henry Parker," in a rush. "My father was Henry Parker."

"Quieter, Henry."

"But not junior. Momma didn't like that on account the boss man was called Junior. Henry Two is what they call me."

"Slow down, Henry Two. You talk like you're falling downhill. I'm Cal." He extended his hand.

Henry did not take it. "If it's all the same to you." Cal wasn't offended.

"You're right, my hands aren't very clean. I like to use water to clean my hands, don't you? George has our water." Cal scooped at the earth and rubbed his hands together with dirt and rocks.

Talking to me like I'm his friend, Henry thought. I did save his life. Henry smiled. "I could use some water."

"Thank you Henry Parker Two, for saving my life. And you'll have water and hardtack and a pillow tonight. One thing. George, the big guy. He's blind, Henry. Can't see. And he is bad around death. Understand? Tell me about how you got here. That was a grave?"

And then Henry Two sobbed, and shouted, and cried more, and Cal gripped his hand, and Henry sorely wept. George was right there, and understood enough, knelt, and the boy buried himself in Thunder's chest and was enveloped in the arms of the giant.

@@@

Henry told them all of it, what he had seen.

The giant Huntred and the legless boy Straw had "gone exploring and gotten lost" the day and night before, and had returned to the regimental encampment with a horrific story and a small child, a survivor of the murder of a runaway slave family. The soldiers' unauthorized absence was forgotten.

Colonel Time and First Sergeant Kuriger were staring into a small but efficient fire the next evening, having listened to the soldiers' and child's rendition of the events. Time and Kuriger knew of evil, and had lived close to it. Some evil could never be comprehended. The actions of the one called Dogtooth were long rumored, and were as evil as it gets. They separately and silently vowed to eliminate such a person from the living. The one called Redbeard was known by every soldier in both armies as a ruthless, mindless murderer, who seemingly tortured and killed simply for the sake of it.

"Sir, let's keep the found boy close by. He can tend to your horse." Kuriger spoke to the colonel when he saw fit, as Time did not care for unnecessary protocol.

"His father's impulse in stopping that scum in the infirmary was a most noble act, and cost him his, and his family's, life. Redbeard and Dogtooth are too close for comfort." Time's jaw clenched.

"We have to look out for those two, Colonel. They'll see us as weak, as easy pickings," said Kuriger over the crackling flames.

Time was clinical. "I know this Redbeard. We must do more than look out. The army must actively hunt him down. Yes, a weak response from the threat of these men begs a stronger action from such evil. We must kill them; no capture, no trial." Time spat, then looked at the stars. "Good is a force, sergeant, when exercised justly. Evil can only be kept at bay, and is never completely defeated. When necessary, evil must be crushed without pity."

"Makes it always necessary to me, sir."

"Abram." Colonel Time had never used Kuriger's first name before, though they had eaten and slept and fought shoulder to shoulder, together in body and spirit, for over ten years.

"The right thing might not be easy, but wrong is always wrong. We kill those bastards as soon as we can."

"Yes, sir."

@@@

Dearest Mother,

I know the writing is not my own, but by my good friend Caleb Straw, who is penning my words spoken to him today. My hands are fine. My body is whole. I have had an accident that has made it difficult for me to see in the light of day, and small figures are somewhat blurred.

Caleb writes for many of us, his writing script is beautiful I am told. I am sure he makes corrections so we say what we want to mean. We ache all the time but we ache together. My work may be boring to some but I am glad to do it, and am called upon to lift great things or laugh great laughs. Just like when Pop was alive.

He would be proud of me, and ashamed of what the war has done. What has not been burned has been stolen. My only love here is for other soldiers. I do what I can for them and no others. I dream of your face every day.

I cannot express my love for you and for home. I miss you and my sisters and it pains me to think of you. I have not heard from you for many weeks as mail is bad here. I wait for your love in letters.

Most affectionately, your loving son Pvt. George Huntred.

@@@

My dearest sister Maeve, how are aunt and uncle and all our tiny cousins? You did not say in your last letter. You mention a Mr. Hoffman frequently, I do not know him but he sounds like he suits you and if you are happy, I am happy. You did not mention school, but I do pray you are still ambitious and will continue your apothecary study. Yes, perhaps an apprenticeship is in order and uncle can make the necessary introductions.

I am so very grateful for my education. My penmanship is in great demand in our company, and I seem to spend half my day writing letters for others. Please excuse my labored writing, my hands curl. Some of my fellow soldiers talk so fast I cannot write it all down, some cry and sob and one older soldier who cannot read or write clutched his face and head in both hands, and could not be consoled he wept so hard. I wrote then to his wife that he loved her. When he finished spending his spirit, I told him what I wrote, and he told me his wife had died months earlier and he had no one to write to who cared where he was or what he was doing. His children had not survived infancy and he said his wife died of a lonely and broken heart. He said Jesus wept, that it is in the Bible. Then he stood up and limped away.

I cannot write any more today. Praise God I have you to write to.

Your affectionate brother, Pvt Caleb Straw.

@@@

13

Water

★

The Second Battalion's mission after organizing and the float down the Potomac was the guarding of over a thousand rebel prisoners lumped together from units that could not travel north because of disease or infirmity. Colonel Time oversaw every aspect personally. He reasoned that an organized insurrection of prisoners against a battalion of invalids would wreak havoc with battalion morale, the citizens in the vicinity of Belle Plain, the elite of Washington, and the general security of the countryside in Northern Virginia now largely safer from the further degradation of war.

Guarding a thousand prisoners required a site without an easy path to escape, regardless of fencing, wire, or well-placed sentries. A ravine, rocky but subtle, was confiscated from a landowner. Three sides sloped at an angle that would have required much climbing in a concerted effort to escape. The top of the three sides, horseshoe-like, was level, and the fencing that was provided by engineers was sturdy and sharp. The colonel placed three of second battalion's companies at the top, an armed sentry every 50 feet, even if seated. The ravine resembled a sugar scoop.

The fourth side, open, sprawled to the firm and dry bank of a deep and swift tributary, and was the logical path for escape. Fenced or no, an assault with calculated casualties by determined men would end bloody for the Second, and largely chaotic for the rebels. Time placed three companies here.

The sentry duty at the top was routine, sedentary, and predictably uneventful. Guards would be able to hear the exertion of an escape attempt, and many of the Second were aching to prove they could still shoot.

Sentry duty at the mouth of the ravine was more complicated. Trenches were attempted and abandoned. Ramparts were thrown together with great effort to accommodate the standing, sitting, and prone, with special care for space for those who could not shoot but could load efficiently. Sentries were placed at the fence, but the true deterrent was the sight of dozens of ramparts, interlocking, that would provide a devastating volley of fire over the whole field. The rebels could witness the drill daily. One simulated volley, by a quarter or third of the companies, fifty guns at most, then another within seconds, then another, then another until a keen eye could discern that it took the invalids four volleys to reload the initiating group.

All without commands.

The first day the drill was hourly. This slowed to three times on day two. Guard change had the same effort, silent, and an imprisoned rebel would have sworn that there was an endless supply of capable though disabled soldiers.

In fact, the guards simply changed positions. They rotated from rampart to rampart to breastworks to earthen mound carrying only a weapon, water, and ammunition. The best fortifications were natural, made by God. When men were inclined to try to improve His landscape for protection, they frequently erred. The guards overseeing the confederates from the top of the 'scoop' had fencing and breastworks, were skilled marksmen, and had three sharp angled hills. But Colonel Time knew that the best of prisons would not hold motivated men, driven by hunger, disease, and their collective unknown fate.

The commander of the 18th reasoned that if prisoners held onto hope of decent treatment they would respect their situation and not attempt a reckless escape. Time knew the rebel commanding officer in the camp, a steely-eyed Citadel man of few words and little patience who could be trusted and reasoned with. They had served together in the Plains years before. Time only feared the rogue prisoner.

Colonel Time's breathing became ragged and his hands shook more often by his third day as commandant of the mobile prison camp. The Second Battalion of the 18th Veterans' Reserve Corps was all that remained of his immediate direct command. Kuriger had guided the battalion's execution of the plan for the "river bottom three" companies of D, E, and F. The young officers were nearly incapacitated, save one, Lieutenant William Tecumseh Anderson, who was skittish but alert, only missing one hand. Anderson had devised the interlocking fields of fire plan, the silent rotation of firing rifles to account for reload, and was almost hourly tinkering with the relief, rest, meal and off-duty preparations. Anderson was ambulatory, clear-eyed, and encouraged the older and more seriously wounded with requests for compliance, not ordering, though the soldiers sensed he would have mumbled if challenged.

The men had heard the young lieutenant weep at night. Soldiers cried, some often and hard, but then laughed and attempted something useful, like cleaning a weapon, digging a better seat, or repairing torn gear.

But it seemed as if Anderson was always checking his emotions, crying day and night, a constant stream, and the men of the 18th were shocked at first, understanding at last, but merciless behind the lieutenant's back. When Anderson had introduced himself to his company's first formation, he croaked through every syllable of "William Tecumseh Anderson," and looked at his feet. A soldier with one foot snorted and asked loudly, "Did the lieutenant say William *Teacup* Anderson?"

The laughter was loud, sharp, and ended quickly.

Anderson had looked up, face red from humiliation, angry at himself. Another officer may have ordered the man out of ranks, for a proper dressing down. Another may have told his sergeant to dismiss the men, or may have forced some communal discipline of digging holes, moving rocks, or sweeping dirt. Another officer may have walked away, ignoring all of it.

Anderson stared through the ranks, immobile, a challenge behind his eyes.

"William. Tecumseh. Anderson." He paused. "I will earn your respect. You are dismissed."

Kuriger wasn't there, but it was faithfully and accurately reported to him, and Time was briefed within the hour.

"I can attach myself to F Company, sir," said Kuriger, casually, in a manner he knew Time would probably dismiss.

Time shook his head, smiled, coughed hard, and said, "No, Kuriger, but I can make F my headquarters company. That young man has seen enough brutality. He's still getting used to, to this," and he raised his own crippled hand and smiled again.

Anderson is smart, Time thought, with a sound understanding of a correct defensive posture, and an above average sense of paternal leadership. This young officer he would always try to keep close, whether in a fight or in garrison. Anderson complimented Time's strengths. Time gave Anderson strength. I will keep an eye on this one called "Teacup," he thought; he might not survive without me.

Kuriger knew of the colonel's disposition to young and frightened soldiers, his indulgence toward their fear, and was conflicted. A skittish officer happened, certainly, but most steeled themselves at the first cannon and would rather embrace death than show cowardice. Anderson was no coward, but he was no leader of men in battle, either. Kuriger believed Anderson had earned the name Teacup, as he had seen him when the weight of battle and the unknown of random and heavy fire caused him to be ineffective.

"May I suggest that we assign Old Irish to F?"

Time gave Kuriger as hard and non-committal a look as he could muster. "Fine."

Perhaps Colonel Time saw something of himself in young Anderson, considered Kuriger. Perhaps. If so, then Anderson would be a great officer someday, and soon.

Time and Kuriger had known each other, worked in the same commands with frequent contact, and fought hard in some violent exchanges, here in Virginia, and in Mexico, and in the Plains. If Anderson became half the man Time was now, Kuriger thought, I would march into hell with him.

Within the week, the prison camp north of Belle Plain secure, Kuriger had grown to appreciate Teacup's skill. At least once an hour he had to tell soldiers to refer to the lieutenant by his father's name, not a china cup. It brought amused smiles, but was obeyed. As the days of drill wore on, there were fewer references to the dainty nickname, and a growing proud respect for young Lieutenant Anderson developed. He took care of his men, they said, and we're getting the job done, too.

By the end of the fifth day, Time called for a special messenger, and Kuriger, always close, chose a tall gangly sort whose walk was steady, and could hold his tongue or strike hard with his fist and knew when to choose the difference. The colonel briefed the messenger on his desire for a conference with the imprisoned confederate commander. He spoke deliberately and explained fully his reasoning to the private, who was missing his right hand and his right eye, and had a monstrous wound from ear to crown on that side, which was healing poorly. Time repeated his instructions twice, and then asked the private his name.

"Roberts, sir. Private Charles Roberts."

"Private Roberts, what are your orders?"

"Sir, I am to march at full step to within ten yards of the front gate. I am to announce the following: 'Colonel Bergen, or the commanding officer if he is unavailable, is respectfully requested to meet with Colonel Time, regimental Commander of the 18th Veteran Corps, in ten minutes, here, where I stand.

The colonel requests a response immediately.' And I say this at attention, sir. In my best parade deck voice, sir."

Kuriger interrupted softly, "Sir. 'Respectfully'?"

"Yes."

Roberts was ready, and confident. "Sir, may I speak freely?"

Time nodded assent.

"Sir, what if they ask me questions, or throw things? What do I do? What if this Colonel Bergen says no?"

Time smiled. "He won't. When you get an affirmative response, salute and hold it until it is returned. Once you do that, I will walk out to your position."

Kuriger left the tent, and called out, just above a conversational range, "Officers' call."

There were no runners in the 18ᵗʰ.

All the men were alert enough that care was needed for communication, but yelling and yammering was unprofessional in garrison unless a drill went awry. The calmer the 18ᵗʰ stayed, the calmer the prisoners remained. The method for an officer or NCO call varied by unit, but word of mouth without missing stride was preferred. Everyone knew what everyone would know when it was time for them to know it was axiomatic in any army. The soldiers of the 18ᵗʰ had long before silently agreed that the most important trapping of this militia would be calm.

The three junior officers walked casually toward the command tent. Stinnet's ambling gait was almost comical except for the dignity he bore through his pain, while Rhoads and Anderson were kept in the mouth of the "scoop" because they had no leg injury. This was the soft spot, and Time needed his officers at least able to run. Kuriger motioned his head briefly to the tent's rear, and stood with his back to the prison fence.

"Gentlemen, the colonel will be conferring with the enemy commander. May I suggest that we have our drill now?"

Without a word the lieutenants returned to their respective command posts. Within a minute all guards and weapons were trained on the front gate.

We can't be too careful, Kuriger thought.

Private Roberts burst from the command tent and marched purposefully, back arched, weaponless, toward the front gate. Stopping as planned, he made his announcement to a passive and hostile wall of fenced in prisoners.

Silence. Just as suddenly shouts from the gate, men running but controlled, then in a few heartbeats, silence again. A runner came to the fence from the depths of the prison, and whispered to one older prisoner who was given a wide berth by all.

That cadaverous rebel, in rags, eyes hollow, voice of gravel, then stated with false solemnity, "The colonel will come forthwith." His gaze never left Roberts, but looked up, down, and up again. Hard not to stare at that head wound.

Roberts was aghast. He had not been this close to a mass of rebel prisoners, and he believed they looked like walking dead, in tatters. He slowly rose his finest salute, arm sharp, all the right angles, palm flat. His left arm.

More prisoners began to walk to the fence. They stared at Roberts, who held his salute, keeping at rigid attention, eyes straight. The prisoners, though quiet, began to move with more curiosity, then purpose, and then yielded to an unseen force.

The old rebel who had spoken gestured at the breastworks behind Roberts, and barked at the growing phalanx of prisoners, "You'll be stayin' right here, boys. Move aside."

Then to Roberts, "The colonel will be here in a moment."

Then back to the mob that almost crushed the fence, loudly, "Move aside!"

Colonel Bergen was cutting a path through the sea of men. He saw and felt their collective condition and ground his remaining teeth, all six of them, all on the left side. His men had fought bravely for years, and many of this one thousand had been with him from the beginning. Less than half were with him at Rappahannock this past November, kept constantly and unnecessarily on the move. The futility of his position was too overwhelming to dwell upon. Most of the other prisoners were stragglers, and the vital soldierly core of his fighting command was long dead.

Bergen had surrendered at Rappahannock, and had watched helplessly as his men had slowly died before his eyes over the past half year. Disease was a certain though not swift death. Hunger took longer. The occasional scuffle brought injury and infection and more death. Escape had been attempted numerous times, always with disastrous results. Always. The union did not publicly execute for attempts. They just made it less attractive than a benign wasting of time.

Bergen spoke something to the old rebel.

Time marched past Roberts, directly to the gate, stopping at arm's length from it.

"Colonel Bergen, will you accompany me?"

The rebel commander kept his frozen stare riveted on the union commander's chin. None of the prisoners moved. A distant call from a hawk echoed throughout the camp, and Bergen waited until the bird's cry died before speaking.

"Greetings, Colonel Time. I request, by your leave, that we conduct our discussion here."

It was an unexpected request, and Time gave it quick thought. "Granted, sir."

The small show of respect to the fallen commander was the least he could do, Time thought; Bergen is probably wary that he may be permanently separated from his men. That would be Time's concern if the roles were reversed.

Bergen rose his head slightly, chin up, and his sparse malnourished frame rocked back as he squared his shoulders. He raised his left hand slightly, and cocked his wrist, and let it fall slowly back to his side.

Roberts, still in position behind Time, dropped his salute and remained at attention.

Without a word the rebel prisoners withdrew, eerily silent, moving with their backs to the fence, well out of earshot. The older rebel, much older than his revered colonel, remained four steps away, alert.

"Colonel Bergen, I think you can see there has been a change of the guard. Do not assume that these men are incapable. I believe the drill over the past few days has demonstrated their discipline and professionalism."

Bergen's smile, mostly gums, while trying to display the remaining teeth on his left side, appeared sinister.

"My compliments, Colonel Time. I suspect that at this stage of the war, our confederacy is doing the same with the able and willing."

"I caution you not to take advantage of the situation, sir."

"I caution you not to threaten me, sir."

Neither commander wavered. Bergen spoke first.

"I will not organize an escape, and I will discourage, uh, 'taking advantage' of your Veterans' Corps. Yes, I know of your formation and command of the 18th. Our prison is not as isolated as you think, Colonel. And your troops are not very secretive."

Bergen paused, but was not finished.

"I need better access to fresh water. Our latrine is inadequate, and without tools to dig we will all be sicker than hell soon. You can't dig our holes, colonel, I can see that. Let us take care of ourselves, and we will respect your position. We could use clothing, linens, rags, anything. As you can see, our uniforms are falling apart, useless."

Bergen raised both arms, outstretched, and for an instant Time thought he was mimicking the crucified Savior. Just as suddenly, Bergen let his arms fall back to his sides.

Time saw the request for what it truly was: a plea masking a threat. If the rebel prisoners could not improve their lot surviving in the camp, they might choose their death through a breakout. The attempt would have heavy casualties. Companies A, B, and C had orders to rain fire on the masses of prisoners from the top of the horseshoe plateau in the event of an escape alarm. At the mouth of the scoop the three companies Time was embedded with could begin their volley and reload defense with some practiced skill, but as each drill perfected the routine, the rebels were sharpening their counter offensive plan. More rebel casualties, certainly, but an able-bodied starving prisoner with nothing to lose would be a formidable opponent for any soldier, not to mention a crippled one. Time estimated that he would lose over 80% of D, E, and F companies, if not all. The 18ᵗʰ would likely be overrun, or worse, would surrender.

"Agreed."

Relieved and unguarded, Bergen let his shoulders fall slightly. "Praise God."

"Roberts."

"Yes, sir!"

"Summon First Sergeant Kuriger."

"Colonel Time," said Bergen, almost as an after thought, "If your brother is still with us, please give him my compliments."

Time offered a thin smile. "I pray your family is safe, Colonel Bergen."

@@@

Kuriger came at a gallop, partly to show that one hand did not remove his vitality, and largely because of Roberts's urgency. As Time briefed him on what was expected to be arranged, Bergen gestured the old rebel forward to the fence. Kuriger did not show his own skepticism, his reservations buried for now. Soon these men could be my neighbors, he thought, this is their land, too. But I cannot trust them yet.

The old rebel, a Sergeant McArdle, had a keen eye for efficient work detail, and was proud to be able to have his men doing something productive to improve their collective condition. Shovels and picks were to be inventoried and handed out. There would be no guards within the camp.

Tools were returned before dark, and redistributed after dawn. From the top of the horseshoe, guards assigned themselves to look specifically at a tool in a prisoner's hand, as it was easy to focus on the product of diligent and useful labor. Each guard was now watching his former self. *I shall never use*

*a pick like that myself, ever again. I used to curse that work, now I
cannot imagine doing it. I could not even dig my own grave.*

Although the rebels were gaunt, they were able-bodied
and threw themselves into the work. Most rebel amputees had
died in futile anguish long ago. Conversation was becoming
more obvious between guards and prisoners, even though
the officers and NCOs discouraged it through example by
only issuing formal questions and one word answers. Burial
details were daily, mass graves dug by prisoners. Latrines
were covered and dug elsewhere. Prisoners offered to dig
new latrines for the 18th, and were stonily told no.

Water and bathing privileges at the river were given,
groups of five for five minutes each, during daylight. Bergen
estimated he could have the entire regiment bathed in under a
week if a rogue soldier did not disrupt the fragile trust.

It is every soldier's duty to attempt escape, which was
second only to his duty to obey his chain of command. Bergen
and McArdle had put the word out, emphatically, that if there
was an escape attempt, it would put the whole camp back
to its previous hellish position. If the union guards don't kill
you, McArdle spat, I just might.

Even the most hardened soldier, no matter how wretched
his lot, will succumb to the kindness of dignity conferred, and
a trust in human nature develops, silently agreed upon and
formalized through small reciprocal behaviors. The guards of
the 18th fared little better than their prisoners, even in food
and tenting. Tents especially were in short supply, and half the
men in Time's command did not have them. The rebels saw
this and did not make demands for them. Both sides suffered
from chronic fatigue, exposure, and malnutrition. The toll on
the 18th was as profound as it was on the prisoners. The men
of the Veterans' Corps were imprisoned by their limitations,
the only difference from the rebels being the 18th was largely
unburdened by hate.

By the fourth day after the agreement, the newness had
faded, the disorganized politeness had vanished, and the
heaviness of respective roles slowed down the pace of activity.

Even the trips to the riverbed slackened in enthusiasm. The sickest prisoners, through disease or hunger or injury or depression, had less to look forward to and did not relish the coolness of the clear crisp water.

The unsteady tranquility would not last after dawn on the fifth day. A scuffle in the prison camp erupted before the first thread of light fell on the gate, and the cry was enormous and anguished from within the prison compound. Three rebels had feigned starting a work detail early. Both union guards and confederate NCOs had slackened their respective intensity and were sleepy-eyed when the cry of "Halt" went up from within the camp.

A hawk flying above would observe uniformed men in a permanent prison of their physical deformity, whose spirits were high. The imprisoned men west of the fence were in a temporary hell, consumed with simple survival. The savvy rebel soldier would be able to wait this one out. It was their land, too, after all. But the indignity of being a caged man in a cesspool was too much to bear for a few, who could not see any wisdom in waiting.

The gate was quickly breached; the three rebels bolted the level ground to the river. Once they passed the first breastworks, their chances improved. The guards were now turned around and firing in close quarters was too hazardous to risk. The shock in the pre-dawn light was disorienting for those on duty, now accustomed to loose standards of the watch. The rebels ran as if through sand, weakened by their physical state but propelled by the smell of freedom or death. Their goal was the river. The guards could not make chase even on level ground, and would not pursue in the flow of the Potomac. The sentries atop the horseshoe could see little and their fire was held.

An older union soldier, the one called Old Irish, missing a foot, had just completed a watch, stretching with his blouse unbuttoned, when he heard the first yell from the camp. Sipping a cup of hot water to warm his head and his hands, he dropped it and reached for his rifle not more than a hop away.

In standard garrison, when not on watch, troops stacked their arms, tee-pee like, for safety and retrieval and accountability. Old Irish did not believe he was in garrison, surrounded by thousands of miserable rebels, and used his rifle to effect as a cane for short walking trips.

He always had his rifle, though he sometimes neglected his canes. A matter of value, he guessed.

The light quickened in the cloudless morning, reflecting off the river. He was thirty yards away from the running men, who were moving directly across his line of sight. No one was firing, though there was much yelling and pointing. No weapon was shouldered anywhere. The hollering became more urgent. Several guards attempted to give chase with great effort but little effect. The invalids moved as if through mud.

"Always ready, dear, always."

Paper, ball, punch, thumb and eye the flint. . .

Old Irish was proud of his marksmanship, and had no qualms or hesitation about his duty now. He knew instinctively that if these men escaped without consequence, then a thousand prisoners would make for the river, whether they could swim or not. And possibly take a few union souls to hell with them on the way.

He steadied his weapon, he now rigid on one leg, judged the distance between each man, tracked the first runner, watched the second pass his field of vision, and fired.

The third prisoner fell hard, pitched face first, legs dug in the last strides, back bent forward, immobile. The other two never looked back, made the river, jumped in, and ran and swam and the current took them away, two black balls floating on the surface, out, out, and then wholly from view.

When the shot was fired and the rebel fell dead the silence of man cut through the screams of a thousand birds who took flight crying and calling out having been shocked into migration. The flock moved as one from the trees at the base of the hill, east to the river, curled west to the prison camp, screaming, circled and flew further west out over the horseshoe and out of sight, the cry echoing and dying.

Kuriger's commands were heard above the din, orders to train weapons on the gate, secure all work parties, full alert all hands, man the breastworks.

The imprisoned rebels stared at the river, wishing the two escapees survived the flow, knowing that they themselves would not touch it again for awhile, perhaps for the duration.

Old Irish knelt by the fallen prisoner.

"Very dead. May God have mercy on your soul."

The one-armed cynic Messerel called out, "Not much in the way of honor, now, right Irish?" It was loud enough for it to carry to the rebels who stood by the gaping hole in the fence, who could have all made it to the river, to freedom or death.

Irish sprang up, wheeled, and spat, "Let others talk about honor. I shoot 'cause I can, 'cause the army will feed me and not shoot me. I fight so I can go home with only one hole in my arse. I shot this man for you." He pointed and glared at the rebel line, those slumped and defeated. Irish locked eyes with Bergen and McArdle, who stood in front of the mass of prisoners.

"If that means I have to shoot every one of you bastards, so be it." He hopped on his good foot, and used his rifle to help him stumble to his canes a few yards away. Damn them for making me do this, he thought, and looked out to the birds gliding away smoothly over the river.

@@@

Mother and Father,

We've just moved a short distance away from the Potomac. Our Corps was guarding thousands of rebel prisoners and three tried to escape. One was killed with one shot by an older soldier who we call Irish but no one knows anything about him. He talks all the time and will opinion about everything from trout fishing to church building but we know nothing about him. He has one foot. He might not even be Irish.

We may be on the march again soon. We floated down the river weeks ago laughing and being sick and miserable and now we have to walk to another camp in another dying town filled with army. I have thought of coming home. I cannot. If I ever saw one of the 18ᵗʰ one year or thirty years from now I wouldn't be able to meet his eye if I left my post now.

Every day I learn something I can do and something I cannot. Missing a limb is bad but I am not dead. Praise God. I love you all. I think of you when I rest.

Your devoted son, Cpl CC Perks

@@@

14

Deed Unpunished

★

*N*ight ended but the day had not begun. An early fog shrouded the encampment, weaving itself into the trees. The air was moist but cool. The sun never stood a chance of breaking through. The fog resisted its ascent, crushing itself into the earth, leeching onto trees, tents, weapons, men and mud. Sound was muted, as if a bowl of cotton was placed over the battalion. Men moved slower. If there was speech, no one heard it. On occasion metal hit metal, as if accidently, and the clink stopped, without reaction. Horses snorted and bayed, necks slick, snouts wet, spewing droplets of dew. They pawed, hooves poised above the ground, lightly, as if testing the lengths of their own legs.

Men slept or stared, at horses, trees and fog. Men awaiting orders. Men yearning for purpose but content to sit. Men anxious for a plan. Men agonized over loss, in pain, doubting they were missed by those they loved.

A week after the escape attempt, the Second Battalion was relieved of its guard of the prison, and ordered to march the able to Port Royal, nearly 25 miles south of Belle Plain. The 18th was to move on foot, without a wagon train, and would be assigned to guarding supply stocks, not men. The Second was bivouacked near its departure point, a half mile away from the prison and the water.

The day before the march was marred by the necessary but cruel consequence of punishment toward a desperate man.

The remnant of a split rail fence, four sections of six feet each, starting true as if challenging the earth to dislodge it, shone burnt umber in the cotton blanket of fog. Each section ran inexorably and inevitably toward the earth, until the last section merged at an angle into the ground. The fence's blade-like arc toward the earth never lost its color, in stark contrast with the grass around it and the soldier tied with rope, arms spread, to its higher cross rail. It appeared that the union soldier had driven the fence downward by his own weight rather than being a prisoner of it.

He sat in low grass, legs spread. His head moved from side to side, lower than his shoulders, a full beard seemingly keeping his mouth from opening on its own. The soldier was missing his left hand, his tunic the original light blue faded and filthy, now dusty grey. The left sleeve was empty and unpinned. The rope on the left arm was tight, and high near his shoulder.

He had stolen a ration of hardtack, the most tasteless and sacred food staple of the army, from another soldier. He could have asked for more from any one of this company. He chose not to, but took it, and then tried to deny the theft. Stealing in close quarters is rarely fruitful, and soldiers have their own code for bold thievery, especially for less than honorable, selfish reasons. Some would have been satisfied with shooting the man. Stealing food from a blind man was bad business in the Veterans' Corps.

George could feel the cold blanket of fog, and could smell the thief a dozen yards away. He could not picture him, and did not know him. The thief was very quiet, and had never spoken directly to George, or he would have remembered. But he could smell his filth, his rancidness, his resignation.

The soldier turned thief had been hit hard about his face and head by the men who caught him. His jaw was swollen, nose flattened, and one eye closed. Still his head lolled from side to side, slowly, to an unheard cadence. His upper jaw was hard, reddened, and dry. The abscess above his gums, beneath his eye, grew slowly and inevitably. The pain was eased only by the rhythmic roll of his head and neck, as if motion could stop the tide of infection growing under his cheek.

He opened his mouth, the pain shrieking within him, as a slow murmur passed from his lips. His tongue darted, swollen from thirst, and then receded. He could endure no more.

A croak, a whisper. "Thunder."

The legless boy slept soundly, as did most of the company. But George heard the thief clearly.

He trained his ear, thinking it may be his imagination, and then heard it again.

"Thunder."

George was moved by, and moved to, the sound. The stench intensified. All soldiers smell bad, but this one had shat himself. There was infection in the air, too, the smell of human rot. All smells were more acute for George. It's one reason why he didn't laugh anymore.

Crawling on all fours, George drew to within a body length of the thief.

"What's your name?"

"Pull my too'." A rasp, choked. "*Hur-wy.*"

George moved until his hand grasped the thief's leg, and then patted up to his hip, then chest. A thin man, a skeleton. "You could have had my ration if you asked."

"I did. *Hur-wy.*" The skeleton tensed, George enveloping him, straddling his leg while kneeling, both hands on the thief's head. The thief opened his mouth and the stench was overwhelming. George gagged, tried to control it and wretched dryly, twice.

George forced his left hand into the right side of the thief's mouth, two fingers knuckled and curled.

The skeleton moaned, low, tears and snot streaming down his face into his open mouth and beard.

"Tha'," through the open mouth, "High."

George's left hand was firmly in the thief's mouth, and he could feel gums and gapped teeth, small and jagged. He wedged his knuckles until he had the safest purchase. George found the middle of the thief's upper lip with his right hand, his first two fingers, gingerly, finding only gums. The stench from the thief was monstrous.

"*Hur-wy.*"

George gently traced his fingers, slowly to his own left.

"Unh unh unh." A negative signal. George quickly and tenderly moved to his own right, past where two or three teeth should have been, and touched it.

The thief heaved, tensed his head and neck, and fought for control. If he could, George would have seen a man whose undamaged eye bulged in pain, in terror that the agony in his head would never abate.

George smelled the skeleton's rot and desperation. He pinched the tooth, hard, and tried to pull. It slipped through his fingertips, and did not give. The thief started shaking, neck and head rigid in pain, legs flailing, still silent.

"I canna help you if you move. I have no knife with me."

"*UHLL IT.*"

George tried again, and the thief thrashed and spasmed in pain. George leaned back, removed his left hand bracing the jaw, and then thrust his left arm behind the thief's head, gripping him powerfully, raising his knee and planting it in the thief's chest, pinning the man, who grew more spasmodic, and nearly uncontrollable.

The skeleton's groan began, pent up from days of pain and thirst and hunger, unable to quell or quiet. The morning peace tore like a sheet, and camp sounds enveloped them. George heard the man's roar of pain as his final act, and thrust his right hand back into the thief's mouth.

"Dear God let this tooth come now give me Your power to help this wretch please please please."

George gripped the tooth, dug his fingers into the gumline, placed his thumb behind it, felt the jaw clench, his own fingers bitten and gummed, as the jaw opened and the thief howled, and he dug deeper.

"Thunder, stop."

"George, no."

"Don't do it."

The troops nearby had heard and looked and assessed and assumed the worst. They hesitated, but the howl of the thief compelled them to pull George off the man. Blood gouted, George's right hand holding a tooth. The thief's head hung low; he did not move.

"What have you done?"

"He killed him."

George tried to crawl back to the restrained skeleton.

"Is he dead?"

"Why's he holding. . ."

George, first too shocked to speak, came alive.

"He called me to pull his tooth," and he held it up. The crown was jagged, filthy, and greenish. The roots were clean and bloody and white.

Sergeant Kuriger strode into the group ringed around George, who sat sprawled on the ground, holding up the healthy tooth.

Kuriger understood immediately.

"Go get the doctor. Move, now."

And two soldiers ambled off as fast as limbs and canes could take them.

Kuriger knelt at the thief, opened his mouth, and gagged. He saw the clean hole, the blood oozing, and he also saw the abscessed tooth, still embedded next to the hole. Much pus had mixed with the blood, been swallowed in fear and pain and futility. The thief had vomited when George had yanked the wrong tooth, and drowned in it, quickly.

"Dear God." He slowly dropped the man's head to his chest, a last decent act.

Kuriger had seen an abscessed mouth before, and knew that it could kill the strongest of men. He had seen many more gruesome ways to die, but suffocation was still miserable.

He looked at George Huntred, whose wide scarred and shut eyes stared at blackness, head darting left and right, while holding up the bloody tooth, searching for approval, like a loyal hound might plaintively wait for his reward.

"Private Huntred. The man here is dead."

"Nooooooo."

Kuriger put a hand on Thunder's shoulder.

"You tried. He was going to die, the rot was too great. You could have pulled all his teeth, and it would not have saved him."

The doctor arrived, looking first at George, and then knelt at the dead soldier still tied to the rail.

Kuriger announced to the developing crowd, "All of you, to your breakfast. We are moving to Port Royal in an hour. Corporal Perks, get a burial detail for this soldier." A pause, "Thunder."

"Yes, sergeant, yes, what. . ."

"Stand up, come with me."

Kuriger gripped Thunder's elbow as they walked, the giant keeping his stride to shuffle-like steps. He trusted Kuriger's judgment, but Cal was his eyes for walking. Thunder told Kuriger so.

"Now tell me what happened."

George recited without hesitation all his movements and motions, his reasoning, his anxiety and then his overwhelming guilt.

"I'll have none of that, private. You tried to help a fellow soldier. You used your best judgment. He called to you, specifically you. You did your best. He was already dying. None of us knew."

Kuriger had allowed the thief to be tied to the fence after the theft. He had always thought him a coward and a cheat and a liar. He saw righteousness in that he was dead.

Thunder would not speak for many hours, and then only to Cal.

@@@

Dear mother, I have seen dreadful things that happen in war, the rage of man killing man, but I cannot forget the cruelty of the human condition right where I sleep.

A soldier caught stealing was tied to a fence yesterday as we have no jail in the field, and most of us cannot walk fast or shoot worth a lick. He deserved to be tied like an animal as I never trusted him ever. A big blind soldier tried to help him or hurt him but the thief choked and died on his own spit up, an ugly and not a good death that happened fast but seemed to take forever. I watched it, and could not understand and then I could not help him it was too late.

I will always rest on my side. I have been shot at and clubbed and cut all over and left for dead but I cannot bear the end of choking on my own vomit.

Your son, Paul Musgrove

@@@

Part Three

The March

"Though I walk into the midst of dangers,
You guard my life when my enemies rage.
You stretch out Your hand;
Your right hand saves me."

Psalm 138:7

15

First Day

★

The march to Port Royal began with 166 men. The regimental doctor found 161 men fit, and five officers refused to be examined, including Colonel Time, he alone on a horse. Most men carried less than five rounds of ammunition. All had water for one day, rations for two. Coffee and tobacco were the only luxuries tolerated, to a man, and pencil and paper were most rare. All had bayonets or large knives. The 18th may not be capable of assault, but they would fight like devils in close quarters. They were suited for defense only. Socks, handkerchiefs, and bandanas for neck and brow were pooled and shared.

The doctor informed Time he wanted to walk the 25 miles, but a head cold was making his chance at success small. Most of the terrain to Port Royal was flat. It was the rain that concerned him. Incessant, unpredictable and unforgiving in its misery. As soon as boots seemed to dry, hats had more sweat than water, trousers stopped chafing hidden parts, and the rain would return. The chafing hurt those one-legged more than their crutch under the arm, and teeth gnashing was the most familiar sound of pain. Those with two legs helped those who limped on one. Those with one leg wiped clean the faces of those with one arm. The doctor's head cold made him the last casualty before the march.

The plodding at the outset was slow but steady. Fifteen minutes of march, hobble, hop, slide, walk. Ten minutes rest. Then march, hobble, hop, slide, walk. Sometimes pull and push. After four cycles and nearly two hours it was estimated that only two miles was covered. By the fifth push new pairings were made, and a pace suitable for all was established. The Second actually picked up strength. Light rain came and went. Crutches and canes navigated the mud better than most boots. The heat dried the path to Port Royal quickly. Double file formation, loose but close, no stragglers, yet all struggled.

The roads were generally firm and flat when dry, and the initial drudgery was complicated only by a lack of foresight. Colonel Time knew he would never make it to Port Royal by sundown. The men had bedrolls, but no tents. The air was humid, thick, and carried the scent of pines, and Time knew that heavy rain was coming. If the warmth held, then at least they would not become incapacitated from exposure. Nearly as bad as death was just being wet.

Inexcusable, he thought. Dear God, what made me think we could do this in one day. I have failed these men again.

"Sir."

"Yes."

Sergeant Kuriger was walking beside the colonel's horse.

"Sir, I can hear you."

Time would have been stricken with humiliation if he wasn't so acutely aware of his own infirmities. He had started involuntarily shaking, his legs, his shoulders, and sometimes his head moved as if ducking from something in flight. It took a Herculean effort to remain close to immobile. I have a palsy, he thought, and now I'm talking out loud to myself. The effort to control his weakened frame was sapping his energy to think clearly.

"I am failing these men. What have I done?"

"Begging the colonel's pardon, sir, but you have failed no one. We," and Kuriger paused for a moment, to let the plural sink in, "thought we could do this in one day. The air is making it hard to breathe. We didn't want to carry tents for they would be too heavy. We are close to fresh water. We have enough ammunition for maybe 4 or 5 volleys. We just need to keep moving."

"Keeping the tents off their backs will seem a foolish indulgence in the pouring rain tonight. No one will sleep."

"Sir, it takes us twice as long to pitch the damn tents. If we had them now we would be leaving men by the side of the road. We canna have stragglers, colonel, there's no one to sweep 'em."

"And we cannot run away," Roberts grumbled to himself, stifling a snort.

Kuriger ignored the intrusion and insolence. Time was less subtle.

"No, you cannot, Private Roberts, but you deserve better judgment from your commanding officer."

Kuriger was slowly boiling. "Sir, these men have nothing to look forward to, but a life as a cripple, a future as an oddity, a living monument to this great and awful war. This work, this march, is their life."

Roberts, though contrite, grew bolder, "We'll remember this march all our lives, sir. This will be an achievement, our achievement."

Time smiled, shook his head.

Kuriger could read the colonel, and knew the damaged man was deeply moved.

"We'll be proud of this day, sir, and talk about it, and tell lies to our children, and hope to God it was not without its purpose."

Time came out of his reverie. "It has purpose, gentlemen. We will be guarding bounty men and supply stocks. It's unlikely we'll deal with prisoners any longer. And we will be self-sufficient."

Fifteen minutes on, ten off. The periods of rest allowed thought to plow deeper into the consciousness, and the absurdity of the formation and mission grew with each relief. After four hours the colonel called a halt. Time dismounted, and motioned Sergeant Kuriger to his side.

"A lot of grumbling, colonel. I think the men would rather push on than rest so frequently. It's almost too wet to eat, anyway," Kuriger half-whispered to Time.

The colonel grimaced at Kuriger. But he knew Kuriger was right. The sooner to Port Royal, the better, he thought, this forced march was ill-conceived. These are good soldiers and I'm punishing the best of them.

Good soldiers, all. His soldiers. Time spoke quickly to Kuriger, "Summon the officers, Sergeant."

The four junior officers were almost there already, the strongest, Lieutenant Rhoads of New York, 4th platoon, was at the colonel's side before Kuriger could dispatch a runner. The companies were now shrunk to platoon strengths, four in all.

The stretch of dirt road was nearly straight, and Time could see the mass of soldiers, 80-odd deep, two abreast. The men must have sensed something as only a handful took advantage of the stop to sit immediately. Most looked side-long or directly at him. Even Henry Two stared expectantly at the colonel, holding his horse's reins. Trenton held steady in the child's hands. Odd. Trenton did not like having anyone except Time hold the reins, and even then it was always a little restless. The blind soldier had that special touch with horses, too. There he is, thought Time, spying the giant with the small one on his shoulders. Even without sight he would be formidable in a close quarter fight.

The officers ringed the colonel. Kuriger behind him, to his left. Henry Two, with Trenton, to his right.

"Gentlemen. I think we've made five miles in four hours. At this pace, we make Port Royal in two days, not one."

The junior offices were dubious. The men did not carry tents, though they always had a bedroll. That meant sleeping in the rain, in the open, with another torturous day of marching, hobbling, pushing, pulling and cursing, and maybe some praying for a swifter end.

Lieutenant Swanson, 1st platoon, at the end of this leg of the formation, spoke first.

"Sir, five miles might be generous. And we are only going to get slower. We'll make it, colonel, but we need a better motivation than just getting there."

Either Swanson read his mind, Time thought, or he is developing a good officer's discernment and judgment. Time waited for others to speak. A breath later he realized that testing his junior officers had a time and place, and this was not one of them. Anderson had two wounds, no right hand, and past images of death overwhelmed his reserves of courage. Rhoads was almost deaf, and was missing his left hand. Swanson was missing a foot and an eye, and was slow to focus. All the men in the company respected Swanson's valor but knew his limitations, and Time saw that value and appreciated him volunteering. Stinnett had lost all his teeth, had a fractured jaw that would not heal correctly, and his back was so wrenched that he walked like he had no knees. Men responded to his stoic visage, and his bearing under great pain made him a model for all. Even with his head bandaged like a beehive.

Now was not the time or place to test them.

Swanson said motivation, and Time knew of only one army motivation short of combat: drill.

"Lieutenant Swanson is right. Our motivation is now immediate. Our standard rules of engagement may not work in these woods, on this road. Marauders can break our line, and try to, well, disrupt us." Time left unsaid that even though the path to Port Royal was considered safe, a concerted attack on the 18th would be disastrous.

Rhoads chuckled. "If bandits are looking for food or ammunition, that's in short supply, sir."

Smiles all around. Time went immediately back to task.

"Let's drill an unknown attack. With our limits on ammunition, fire discipline will be crucial. Food is food, even pieces of hardtack, and at our current pace we may be easy prey. We need to protect what little we have. We cannot incur casualties."

Anderson summed it up for Time. "Maintain unit and line integrity. No chasing ghosts. If there's a breach, the troops will be casualties of mayhem or worse, so holding the line is vital. No unnecessary shooting. Conserve powder for close-in engagement. One shot, one kill."

"Make it count, nothing wasted."

"No chasing bandits into the tree line, probably a trap."

"Hit the ground, face out, fix bayonets."

"Only fire if a clear and sure line of sight."

"Do not give up the line."

The young officers were reenergized and committed to the mission. They fell silent. Kuriger coughed.

"May I suggest, gentlemen, we instruct now, have a thorough understanding, and then tell the men we may "drill" before the next break?"

Time was pleased. "Excellent. Yes, Sergeant Kuriger, a fine suggestion. Gentlemen, return to your platoons and brief them. We move out in five minutes."

@@@

George's breath was steady and deep all morning, but as the air thickened in the mid-afternoon it became shallow and slightly labored. Carrying Cal and two bedrolls, water and food had its effect. George was stronger than a horse, but the passive elements of the summer day in humidity, heat, sun, dust and mud wore him down as slowly and surely as age would take a man years down the road.

The fatigue of being aged quicker by infirmity had its toll on all the 18ᵗʰ on the march. Rain was a mixed blessing. The coolness of water on one's face and neck would be welcomed, briefly. The reality of drenched clothing and unsure footing in puddles and mud would make the ordeal torturous.

They marched on, fifteen minutes of step, slide, hop and ten of a restless rest.

"George."

"Yes."

"We can't be too far now. The colonel will want us to bed down soon."

"I'm fine, Cal. Just tired. I think I can chew the air in front of me," George laughed softly.

Cal tried to bark a laugh, managing only a squeak. He was sore all over. As much as George was conscious of Cal's comfort, every step was a terror and raw wound for Cal, whose guidance was crucial, diligent, and precise.

I can see and react smoothly, Cal thought, George trusts I won't put him in harm. I cannot see unless I lean forward and erect. If I move, he'll move, maybe in error. Must keep my movements short, spare, purposeful.

I cannot walk, he thought, now or ever. Without George, I would be pulled on a cart, or begging for food from a blanket, or pulling myself through dirt and dung and dear God what's to come of me if George. . . he'll not leave my sight, I will protect myself by protecting him. Move less, try to be lighter.

George tried to keep his own breathing steady. Cal's weight was not the problem, nor the bedrolls and supplies of two men. The displacement of the work on a man's back and shoulders was difficult enough under normal conditions, but the heat, the air, the odd bundles of man and gear, and. . .

I'm blind, he thought, I am blind forever. I am shrouded in dark, forever darkness. I can walk now because Cal tells me where to go. But tomorrow? Where will Cal be tomorrow? I must keep him near me, must never complain. I'll be left sightless by the side of the road, begging for food.

"Cal."

"Yes."

"You're my angel. God Bless you."

"Slow a little, lean back some, a few feet downhill. That's good."

"You're my angel."

"And you're mine, George. When we rest next I'll tighten up the pack for us, change your socks. We'll be fine."

"My right hip is sore, Cal, a little raw. Move the gear around some, will you?"

"Yes."

@@@

Rebel cavalry was becoming increasingly rare. Horses were in short supply as the months of the war plodded on. Scouting parties of two years before were large, swift, and able to confiscate much during forays for intelligence or plunder. By the summer of 1864 quality horses had become precious. The demand on both sides was acute. Horses were early casualties in battle. The slightest injury would often prove fatal. Starving men would eat hay at their lowest point, and only the most far-sighted commanders could strike the balance between ensuring beasts of burden and mounted cavalry were both kept to reasonable tactical strengths. Horses could not replace themselves fast enough. The rebels couldn't buy them with ease, as supplies of all kinds were cut off from the Mississippi and the Atlantic. The South was becoming an island. If it couldn't make or grow the war machine, the Confederacy would die.

The South could not grow weapons, and could not breed dead animals. Its offensive had ended the summer before, at Gettysburg. The Confederacy's attack and disperse tactics were running the northern forces all over Virginia, and were largely effective, but as a defense it only prolonged the inevitable in the face of a determined Union Army.

A party of three rebel cavalry rode and cut back and forth without direction through the mid-day heat and humidity, slowly, through the brush south of Belle Plain. The horses were older, stout, and made for cartage, their best years behind them. Carrying a single man was the limit of each beast's capacity. Even in the heat, the rebel cavalry was fully cloaked, crown to knees. Each had a rifle. No bed rolls. Nothing except water sacks and ammunition and empty saddle bags. If not for the snapping of an occasional stray branch, the three riders and horses would appear to be almost still. These cavalry men were not bold or brash or flamboyant.

They had a motivation different than their mission.

The rebel horsemen had strayed far from their appointed rounds, hunger compelling them forward. A day before they were ordered to strike out due east and report by dawn on union encampments, force strength, movement of men or materiel. That would have been twenty hours ago. The thought that they might be considered deserters came to them, and went. Hunger compelled them forward. Bounty was their ticket back to their command. Returning empty-handed was unthinkable.

"It'll rain soon," from the rear, a boy of no more than fifteen.

"It'll cool down the horses," from the second rider, a veteran at the old age of twenty-two.

"Halt," from the leader, a black-eyed, sharp angled soldier, face sunken, whose very posture begged for relief.

"Hear that? A column, slow moving, no wagon train," the leader's exhaustion now gone.

They all heard the same distinct sounds and lack of horses.

"Could be civilians."

"And they'll have food."

The three had not eaten since daybreak ten hours earlier. The horses only had water breaks, and were salting up on their flanks and snouts. The prospect of food, from a poorly defended civilian group concerned more with safety than fighting gave the rebels new purpose.

"Caswell, stay here with the horses."

"Locke, wait."

Locke was leading the mission, but was cross-eyed with fatigue. Liston, the twenty-two year old, wanted to talk this through, have a plan. Leaving the boy Caswell with the horses was not a plan.

Locke was surly by nature, but knew that he had lost effective control of the situation. He was reacting, and poorly. His judgment left him hours before, and only a farmer's back kept him upright in the saddle. His dark eyes bore into Liston, but to no avail. Locke was done.

"Alright, Liston."

Liston moved his hood behind his head, speaking quickly. His eyes were blood-shot, intense and cold.

"We stay with our horses. We don't know where the road they're on goes, or their strength. Could be soldiers, we don't know. My mount still has legs now. The group is moving south. I'll go north, try to determine the rear. You two move slow and right at 'em until you can see a flanking guard or the main body."

"A flanking guard will find us first, Liston," this from Caswell. He pushed his hood back, leaned forward, and dropped his tone to above a whisper, but with the same intensity. "But you're right, we stay mounted. If we have to gallop, even for a short while to take us out of shootin' range, our chances are better." He smiled, pleased.

"You may be right, Caswell, but let's do what I say now. Keep your heads; we can rally here if there's no pursuit," whispered Liston.

"They'll have food," said Locke, flat and simple.

"But they won't hand it to us. I will imitate a fight if I think it will gain us anything, but I'd rather track 'em and wait for 'em to stop. Take 'em from the rear." Liston firmly in command.

"I say we stay together. We split, we put the others at risk," Caswell pleaded.

Locke awoke. "Right, Caswell. But if there's a shootout, or we're seen, outnumbered, we are all in a craphole."

The silence of a few seconds harkened a symphony of forest sounds, wind through leaves, and the rustle of brush, birds, and insects buzzing. The sky darkened, making the three figures invisible in the thickness of the trees. The air grew heavier.

Locke came back to the moment from the recess of his own weariness. "The rain will make the decision for us. I think I hear it coming. As soon as it does, we can pick up our pace. We're gonna hit that line, hard, and take what we can in a rush."

"Damn it, Locke, that's not a plan. We scout it first, then take the rear. The rain will be in our favor, but we still have a job to do. I know you're tired, but you can be tired when you're dead. And I ain't that tired. Is you, Caswell?"

"Hell, no."

"Follow me." Liston took the lead. Locke turned his horse to go second, but Caswell cut first letting his horse go second to follow Liston; Caswell's glare withered Locke right where he sat.

Liston saw the change in Caswell, understood it, but could not countenance disrespect to Locke from anyone else. Caswell was a hairless kid. Once Locke's dignity was stripped he would be worse than useless. He would be as much a liability as a lame horse.

The enemy may put Locke down before I have to, Liston thought.

"Caswell, keep the rear. You stay sharp to the left, away from the road, and behind us. Locke, keep your eye on the road, that flank. I have eyes front, to the rear of their movement. If the rain catches us, we'll pick up the pace. We'll stay together."

The rain came.

@@@

The 18th scrambled and darted, hopped and cursed their way to the sides of the beaten road. The rain fell hard, in torrents, straight down, then sideways, but always hard, the sound deafening.

"Halt" was called and carried down the formation. Nearly all took to a knee or found something to lean or lay on, facing into the surrounding trees.

The rain struck the men like needles, requiring a focus to see never considered consciously before. Most of the men had at least an arm injury, which forced them to carry and secure weapons and goods clumsily. Those with leg injuries could see better, carrying with one arm, wiping their faces with the other, but their movement was workmanlike and slow, as one hand was always dedicated to making a single leg functional.

The rain played tricks, thought Lieutenant Anderson. The storm raged overhead but on the western flank a slice of bright white and blue shown through where the earth met the sky, where the horizon would be if not for the dense pine. There were three large shadows not thirty yards away. They appeared to be large stones, or buffalo, or deformed cattle. He's never seen a real buffalo, and stones don't walk, he thought. Anderson pulled his sidearm and wiped his brow with his stump arm, knocking his hat off.

The sliver of white and blue was gone.

Anderson did not want to shout an alarm, but he was panicked. Did anyone else see anything? He thought he wasn't entirely sure he saw what he thought he saw. Three hooded and cloaked cavalry, may be union, may be marauders, may be rebels.

"Lieutenant." Over the din, that tough New Yorker, Perks. "You okay, sir? You're breathing heavy. You all right?"

Anderson glared at him wide-eyed. Perks had only half his teeth, was missing an ear, and had two cross-hatched scars on his forehead and right cheek. His left hand was missing, and the two small fingers of his right were gone. An able, steady soldier who never complained.

Anderson suspected that Perks had been assigned to watch him. His own eyes grew wide, wider, fighting the rain, thinking that mopping the torrent from his eyes may make him look weak.

"Lieutenant?"

"I thought I saw horses."

"Lieutenant, you can't see squat. Most of the horses in these parts are dead, or pulling wagons, or. . .'

@@@

The rebels' slow walk turned to trot to gallop, and they were still undetected. A prone soldier in a downpour could see little and comprehend less, his infirmity a terrifying reminder that he might not be equal to the task.

Most of the column had taken to a knee, or crouched or knelt on the road's side berm. One solder, Musgrove, stood frozen, looking directly at the cavalry movement.

The rain came harder, shifting, surging, blanketing the visible area. The three horsemen were at a full gallop, but slow in the downpour. No one but Anderson could see as he had tracked them from the small window of light earlier. The cavalry was shielded by trees, brush, and the raging storm.

". . .most of the horses in these parts are dead, or pulling wagons, or. . ." and Perks' head rose a fraction over the berm, staring at the mute Lieutenant, when the lead horse's front hoof imperceptibly creased the side of his head, above his missing ear, cleaving the rough cloth of his hat and then was gone.

Perks, eyes wide, thought first that he had been shot, knowing that impact came before sound before the blood before the pain before incredulity. Anderson moved his hand dart-like to Perks chest, forcing him down, as the first horse and rider leapt onto the road, turning north toward the rear. The second horse was behind, but less forceful. The third stopped short, the ragged snorting of the beast heavy, weakened, unable to exert anything but the power to draw and expel breath. The hooded rider stared open- mouthed at the boyish officer now on the ground, wondering if a man could rest in a stream of mud and running water, wondering why his mount didn't make the short jump down to the road bed and knowing that no, no one can rest in mud, and no, his mount was done.

Locke wheeled his horse gingerly as the other two rebel cavalry forced their mounts to the rear of the column; the raid was fruitless for supplies. The downpour prevented easy theft, and their lack of discipline in the face of hunger to wait out the storm guaranteed failure. Movement meant survival. Only one alert armed soldier would be enough to end this futile mission.

"Damn."

"What."

"FFFF. . . all, we're under attack," shouted Musgrove, standing in a failed attempt to stay dry, couldn't fire his wet weapon, and he swung it like a scythe, clipping the first rider, who was now nearly at the end of the line. It was not enough to unseat the rebel.

The second rider charged Musgrove. His single foot gave, he fell hard, his rifle now invisible in the muck of a deep rut in the road. The horse galloped over him, hooves true to the sloppy earth, missing Musgrove's head by the hand of an angel.

The first rider called out "Go, go, retreat now," spurring his horse through the maelstrom of rain and bodies laying or kneeling or squatting about. Unable to see clearly, fatigue making the discomfort unbearable, the soldiers of the 18ᵗʰ were frozen in alarm almost to a man, watching the hooded horsemen gallop down the center of the column to escape.

All three were gone in seconds.

"Stay where you are, fix bayonets, that could be an advance party," from Anderson, too high-pitched to carry.

"The lieutenant says fix bayonets and be ready," from Perks, who could be heard over the din to the front of the column, nearly a hundred yards away.

The rain came harder. No one moved after fixing bayonet, but no one sat. All were kneeling or prone facing out, tentative questions of "Are you whole?" Any injuries?" Answers "Yes, fine." "No, steady." "Just happy and dry."

"Eyes out," from many, as the rain subsided into a drizzle. Five minutes passed. The threat of enemy or marauders appeared gone. The torment of wet, mud, no means to make a fire, use dry weapons or move freely was worse.

Time came through as quick as the mud would allow Trenton to canter down the center of the formation.

"No one will attack again in this rain. Keep your heads. You have done well." He stayed with the last platoon for several more minutes, and as the rain stopped, he ordered the march to begin anew.

@@@

The rebel cavalry was now a half-mile away, walking their horses over a rocky ridge looking for a path west, southwest.

"Nothing for our troubles."

"At least a hundred infantry. Didn't see a horse. No wagons, no large guns."

"Nothing. No food. Nothing."

"Shut it up. We're lucky to be alive. Our horses have nothing left. They'll have to eat something better than weeds."

"The rain cooled 'em off. The longer we walk, the better."

"Aye. If mine dies, I'll eat it."

"Did you see?"

"Yes."

"All of them."

"Can they be more desperate than us?"

"Maybe. But they weren't ready for a fight. My guess is this was just a troop movement, rear echelon, is all."

"We'll report a loose formation of a hundred to a hundred fifty crippled soldiers, barely able to walk. Armed, though. We had no chance to track longer."

Caswell thought of the lone soldier swinging his rifle at Liston, brushing him. If it connected solid, he thought, and Liston came off his horse, the cripples might have eaten him for dinner.

"Nothing. No food. I'll eat my own hand tonight."

"Shut it up. Find the path home."

@@@

Kuriger estimated the position and determined they were twelve miles out in a little over eleven hours time. It put the troops about halfway to Port Royal. The first opportunity to bed down, he thought, we'd better do so.

"Colonel, the next chance for a level and secure bivouac, may I suggest we take it? I think we'll see no more rebels today."

"Yes, yes, a good idea. I hope the rain holds off."

Behind the column of marchers grey clouds puffed and swirled and meandered cautiously southward, deadheading toward the 18th.

The rain came as a mist.

The column was halted on the colonel's command, and the tree-lined path afforded some relief from the steady drizzle. No one had tents. Bed rolls were made into lean-tos, and two bedrolls provided some cover, to sit under, but not to sleep. The rain ebbed and whipped in the quickening darkness. The 18th began the silent drill of alternating watch and attempting rest by sitting up and then failing at staying dry. There was some relief from not moving, but few would call it comfort.

They were being watched.

Redbeard, Dogtooth and another pair of marauders had paced the marchers for a few miles, from a long distance. The air and heat effected their movement, too, the wind mostly still but occasionally in their faces. The gap in distance was less to do with strategy than convenience. Redbeard had discovered a still, small and crude but with all the potential, freshly abandoned. If the moonshiner or homesteader returned he would find four sour men. Two brothers, dense, filthy, mostly silent, and the ragged beast, Dogtooth, lanky and stooped, who rarely spoke without his hand in front of his face, hiding a single tooth beneath a gnarled lip.

Redbeard, the fourth man, was large and powerfully built. In the heat he wore a woolen overcoat past his knees, black, which made his appearance more foreboding. His hat had been starched at one time, but was now a mess of felt, silk ribbon, and mottled brim. His fire-red beard burst from his head as if trying to escape, or warn the intrepid who dared look him head on.

Redbeard liked the find of the still.

"Dogtooth, get that fire going. It'll rain soon. Hooch and coffee. We're done for the day."

One of the brothers came close. "I thought we'd try to take these boys, the last squad, after a break."

"So did I." Redbeard was loath to acknowledge failure. "The rain will make escape tricky for us. It'll come faster and sooner than I had thought. Not today. Tomorrow. We'll take 'em tomorrow." He was even more averse to disagreement with his word.

The second brother was more than happy to call it a day. "We have liquor, the fixin's for it, some coffee here. This ain't paradise, but it's close."

"There's spirit in the can," said Dogtooth, as an aside.

Two branches snapped simultaneously.

"Don't move." From the brush, even, steady, unpanicked.

"At all." A second homesteader, as steady as the first, also hidden, from a different angle.

Redbeard knew they were flanked on two sides. He did not have to wonder if they were armed, as both men tapped their barrels with an unmistakable clink. Redbeard had his hand near his rifle, but the others were unready. His impulse was to shoot the two brothers for being useless. He would try friendly, first, with these moonshiners or bandits like themselves. He slowly raised his arms upward, even to the ground, palms up.

"Sorry gents, we mean no threat. We knew you'd be back or we would've set up a guard. Forgive our . . . intrusion." Redbeard spoke loftily, rhythmically, extending syllables as if adding syrup to the cake. Casual and confident.

Brother Two had already removed one boot.

Dogtooth stared at the dying embers of the fire he had been coaxing as if entranced.

Brother One slowly turned his head.

"I said don't move," from the brush near Redbeard.

"May I put my arms down, friend?" He smiled.

A rustle from the brush, and a large doughy faced man with an old musket at his shoulder, ready to fire, walked into the clearing.

"Hello, Redbeard. Don't know if you remember me." Then the doughy faced man smiled.

"Well, I'll be." Redbeard, relieved, still kept his arms steady. "Rufus, I can't forget a man who owes me five dollars."

The brothers relaxed and started to laugh.

"Keep it down, boys." Rufus lowered his weapon. "That cripple brigade is on the post road, heading south, probably to Port Royal. We're close enough for gunshots, and maybe just being loud."

Redbeard lowered his arms.

"I'll forget the five dollars for some coffee, maybe a drink. We have some hardtack, not much, but we'll share even."

"Can I re-light this fire?" Dogtooth was frozen over the embers, perspiring heavily.

"Go ahead you ugly bastard." The second man emerged, weaponless. "I scraped my knives together. You boys looked like you crapped yourselves."

The second man, smallish, menacing, hard as a rock, regarded the brothers with open disdain.

"What're you lookin' at?" he asked with contempt, scraping his knives.

"Don't. Touch. Nuthin'," Rufus spat, to Redbeard's crew.

Redbeard now relaxed completely.

"Hey, Farr," he said, to the smallish man with the knives.

"Good to see you, Redbeard." Farr extended his hand, genuinely glad to greet him. "And I don't owe you nuthin'."

They laughed, shook hands hard, and openly gawked at Dogtooth.

"I want to get the fire lit, cousin, then I'll greet you proper."

Farr took charge. "He's right, too much to do. You keep tending to that fire, Dog. Red, help Rufus and me with the lean-to. You two go get more dry wood. The rain will be here soon and it'll be fierce. I'd rather be dry than drunk."

@@@

Lieutenants Rhoads, Anderson, Stinnet and Swanson sat around a small smoky fire, at ease though wet and stiff from the day's exertions. They knew their men needed space, and even though appropriate pickets had been placed, there would be little rest tonight from the vagaries of marauders or scouts for the rebels, and the saturation of all the gear. The officers' fire was just off the road, too smoky like the others, near the center of the formation that stretched lazily for not quite two hundred yards. None of the fires would last long, as the rain made everything wet, and foraging for dry timber was ill-advised. The loose bivouac was quickly encircled in dank smoke.

The harder the men of the 18th tried to normalize their soldierly routine, the sharper their cognizance of the difference. They became more clannish, more resentful of those not similarly afflicted. The standard disdain for junior officers did not extend to these lieutenants, who suffered the permanent physical scars. The enlisted men would not be overly familiar as discipline must be maintained. That was proved again today. License for failures in judgment or courage by these officers were accepted by the men.

But not by Anderson. He stared into the fire, mouth slack, unable to rest. The images of bloody boots, a dying soldier's face, and the sly smiles of derision were overwhelming his conscience and crept into his every waking minute. He heard "Teacup," it seemed, every hour of the day.

"I cannot lead them. I cannot lead myself."

"Nonsense, Anderson." Stinnet rarely spoke, but he was undeterred by his mangled speech. "They want you to lead them. Do not give them reason to doubt. Let 'em call you Teacup; just act like Caesar. If they see you as Teacup, you'll never lead them. They'll forget you exist."

"I am not a soldier. These men are soldiers. These men are better than me."

Swanson was moved by Anderson's agony. He placed a firm hand on Anderson's shoulder. "No. They are veterans. They are fully committed. They have survived. They wish to continue to serve. Their life had meaning before. It has even more purpose now. We cannot take away that purpose. They, we, will serve."

"I lost my hand in an accident," Anderson croaked, "My own mistake. It need not have happened. Why would they follow me?"

"Maybe they need less leadership," said Rhoads, who leaned over the fire to hear better. "They have seen stupidity, we all have. They have experienced the sudden, and seen it up close and slow. We all know now how crucial every second it is to be vigilant, to be careful, to know the objective."

"And to watch one another."

Colonel Time had just emerged from the periphery of the darkness surrounding the lieutenants. The lieutenants started to rise, slowly, and Time curtly and quickly played one hand down, "At ease. Stay seated."

Time had listened for as long as he dared. It was best to keep these discussions loose, but not out of control.

"They want you to lead them. Do not give a soldier a reason to doubt. Be confident in the face of fear. All men fear. Pain, dishonor, failure, death. Know that soldiers expect their officers to show no fear. Gives them a reason not to show theirs."

Anderson looked pleadingly at his colonel.

"They, you, are all different than me, sir, better than me."

"No, just different in their future as can be seen now. Maybe they were better yesterday. But today, now, you are their officer. Set the example. Ignore the ugliness you see. Treat them like the soldiers they are. That is all I ask.

"You young officers must understand that your fear is natural. What will separate you from others is your cool head under fire even when all rational guidance has abandoned the field. You must provide that leadership to achieve the objective, above all. Sergeant Kuriger's job is to bring soldiers home. And he will execute all orders, as he knows that the well-drilled, obedient soldier is more likely to survive than perish."

Anderson pressed on, "Couldn't all this be avoided? Why a war?"

Swanson was emphatic. "I could not avoid going to war any more than I could deny my faith."

Stinnet measured each word: "God made man. Man made slaves."

"And we do this to end slavery; life and liberty are one," stated Rhoads.

Time's eyes widened, impressed by the officers' collective intensity, deepening his tone for emphasis. "Slavery and birth are always woven together. Denying a man freedom is the denial of life. How can we stand by and not allow others to live? Live free? Are children shunned for being born? Are Negroes shunned for existing? These are the same. To deny life is to deny freedom, and denying freedom denies life. It is about life, and liberty, and you cannot have one without the other. All men are created equal. All men. All men. All men. No one decides who can be created, and who should live, except God. Man alone decides on freedom."

Young Henry sat in the darkness, listening, and stared blankly. All men, he thought, except his Daddy. He shuddered to think he could endure more.

Time's palsy was more pronounced, and he coughed to attempt to mask it, and then pushed his campaign hat to the back of his head.

"You must remain brave as officers. If courage fails you, run to the sound. Let the sounds of the fight dictate your action in the absence of orders. A good officer will choose his fight in the face of confusion, and not let the enemy dictate the terms of engagement. A good soldier must keep moving to the sound of battle, embracing the rage and pain in his head."

They all looked silently into the dying and smoky embers. Stinnett and Rhoads each laid extra sticks onto the fire.

"Remember what Milton wrote: '*They also serve, who only stand and wait.*' I don't think your injuries are any more or less heroic or accidental, gentlemen. You survived. You will thrive for the sake of your men. You will do what is required when it comes time for you to act. I have every confidence and faith in all of you." Time walked out of the reflecting light.

Anderson sat straighter. "Beg God this will end soon. We will all be brothers again. Again. God willing."

@@@

Henry Two was quiet. The soldier Perks was always attentive if not exactly kind to him, and offered his bedroll to Henry Two, adding that his watch would keep him up, mind you, but if I'm tired you'll sleep where I put you. He sat on the blanket and stared at the colonel who was in a silent conversation with the dark sergeant, Kuriger. Time appeared to be looking for something on the ground, and Kuriger was unresponsive.

Henry saw what the colonel was searching for: a dull unvarnished wooden cup he always held before he slept. If coffee was not immediately available or offered, he simply held it. It was close to the edge of the light, and an odd reflection made it obvious from ground level, not from standing. Henry darted to the cup, grasped it, and ran to the colonel.

"Here it is, colonel, sir."

Time beamed. "Thank you, Henry Parker. I would not have rested until I found it. And I would be looking for a very long time."

"Why wouldn't you ask the men to look for you, sir?"

"I can find my own gear, son. They have their own concerns."

"But why have them if they cannot be your servants?"

Time frowned, started to go to his knee to talk to the boy, could not, and pretended to be distracted by the small fire Kuriger had built, who acted as if not interested in the conversation.

"Sir? The soldiers are your servants, yes?"

Time sighed heavily.

"Henry, these men serve, but are not servants. They have what is called self-determination. They have largely determined the direction of their lives, if not the full course. They have chosen a path of their own vision, or one shaped by

166

those who care for their unformed character, like a father or mother or brother. Their path is not pre-determined by a false benevolence, one that states, 'Do this and you will be cared for.' The falseness of a man's profit from the indentured sweat of another man's forced labor is not freedom, and does not fulfill the Lord's wish for us. . . to love Him, and serve Him through our own free will. Henry Parker, when people can be bought and sold like animals, by and for others, they are not free. They cannot walk away. Young man, you can walk away now."

"Why? I don't want to!" Henry did not understand conscription or volunteering or the reason for servitude and slavery, and comprehended even less of what Colonel Time spoke.

"You are a child, Henry, no longer any man's property. You are first and always a child of God."

"I want to stay with the soldiers, colonel!" Henry had seen little of God recently.

"Well, Henry, if you choose to stay, it must be as a soldier. Will you take an oath to serve the United States Army?"

Henry Two stared intensely, jaw rolling, eyes brimming, wanting to speak but not knowing what to say. He understood little of the great colonel's thoughts, but knew enough that he had to commit to something, now, or be forever alone.

"I want to be in your army, sir. I want to be a soldier."

Kuriger stood. "Now is a good time to stand and salute your commanding officer, Private Parker."

"Yes, sergeant! Thank you, sir!" And a damn fine salute it was.

@@@

Rhoads, Anderson, Stinnet and Swanson had looked into the smoky fire in silence for many long minutes, engrossed in their own thoughts.

Men speak casually in the dark as if to themselves alone, even when surrounded by others. Soldiers only listen to what they want to hear when not on duty, staying immersed in their own beliefs, reluctant to explain, open to agreement, and on occasion looking for a confrontation. The officers of the 18th avoided disagreement, challenging little of what was discussed openly, being agitated or content in their own thoughts.

"Have you considered why, why all of this?"

"To smite evil. For good and forever."

"Are we fighting against evil?'

"Should all men be free? Men are not cattle! Men are not horses! Owning another is evil!"

"If we submit to evil, just allow it to grow, that is wrong. But if evil takes you, God will protect you, here and hereafter."

"We should hold some things even above our honor. Like the Declaration says: life, liberty and the pursuit of happiness. If we aren't fighting for liberty for all, then we have nothing."

"And like the Bible says, *'no longer a slave, but more, a brother'*."

"I know that one, Philemon, true enough."

"But life comes first. Without it nothing else matters. Scores are killed by the minute. For what?"

"You sound like an old woman."

"For truth. This is truth: men should not own other men."

"There's a certain fairness in being free."

"Death isn't fair."

"None of this is about fair. It is about justice." This from Anderson, who had not spoken yet.

"But this death around us is so. . . mindless, so meaningless."

"It is not that dying makes life meaningless, or that being alive makes it less so. I must make my life mean more. Only I can do that," said Anderson flatly.

The others stared at him.

Rhoads said loudly, as if the others were nearly as deaf as he, "I think we'll remember this march for a long time."

Swanson rubbed his stump leg. "I may remember this march the rest of my life, but it took all my life to get to right now, to tomorrow's memory. I do suspect that I'll recall mostly what my life was like before, with both feet."

Hours later, after the fire died and the men were huddled and curled in an attempt at sleep, the air warmed slightly, the wind died completely, and a dryness kissed the brows of the 18th.

Anderson had a different dream this night.

Waters swirled in a large basin and he struggled to submerge himself, while he knew that keeping his head above the tide was crucial to breathe. He gulped for air, while still fighting to lower himself into the roiling mass. He slipped into the black surf and slept soundly and fully.

@@@

Cal slept deeply and happily dreamt the same images again.

Delaney was working linens and bedpans and cool rags for the bedridden. Cal was in an infirmary, and she had followed him there, while early in his convalescence, hoping to look after him. She stood at the foot of his makeshift bed, more comfortable than the table at the farmhouse had been. Delaney couldn't take her eyes off the boyish face in slumber, his mottled blond hair, flaxen like hers.

Cal fussed, sensing the attention. He opened his eyes in the dream, blinked rapidly, and shot his lids open. He started to smile, opened his mouth in shock, and then thought to feign sleep. He tore his eyes away, and then slowly turned back to Delaney.

Her gaze never wavered from him.

Cal spoke to no one, but prayed that the girl would talk to him. Her big toothy smile and slender limbs made her look smaller and younger than her years.

"If you love me you'll be happy forever," Delaney sang above a whisper.

"I'm looking for my legs."

Her smile became a thin line. "You have legs. They just don't reach the ground."

He smiled back, meeting her gaze. She glowed like an angel.

@@@

16

Second Day

*T*he new morning's reveille to prepare to march was sharp, and quick, and each man possessed a renewed purpose. Old Irish, true to acting independent, staying close enough to keep an eye on Lieutenant Anderson, broke out in a wild riotous cadence without rhyme or direction. After a few steps of shuffle, hobble and hop, it was painfully apparent that his boisterous spontaneity was nothing more than relief at moving, and the irregular laughter could be heard clearly by the colonel over eighty yards away.

Time smiled. Although the clouds threatened, the air cooled, and he guessed there would be no rain for a while. Providence in the form of cooler air lifted the 18th to a step they had not previously possessed as a unit, harkening back to days not so long ago when they were soldiers, with all their faculties, eager to fight, enthused to engage the enemy, marching into immortality for the sake of Old Glory.

Old Irish's ditty continued, the laughter died away, and each step, shuffle, and hobble accented the pain that the 18th was no more a fighting unit than a gaggle of children walking home from school.

Henry Parker Two kept at the march, striding with soldierly purpose, arms swinging high, glancing at the brave colonel on the magnificent Trenton every other step. The very young embrace routine with no cynicism for monotony.

He needs a man's approval, too, Time considered, just like my soldiers. Just like his father might have approved. On impulse, Time called to Henry Two and asked if he would like to ride, also, above the horn on his saddle. He was light enough, a cloth doll of a child.

Young Henry needed no encouragement. In two steps he was at the colonel's stirrups, dangerously so, and reached both arms up as if asking his Daddy to carry him, expectant, trusting. Time reached with one gloved hand, grasping the boy under his arm, and was struck by how frail and thin he was. Gracefully, as if he performed the trick a thousand times, Henry swung in front of Time, and perched himself above the saddle horn on the horse's neck, smoothing his hands on each side of the beast, which didn't break its soft canter.

"Well done, Private Parker."

The child turned, beamed, and squeaked, "Thank you, sir!"

"Today will be a grand day for the 18th, Henry Parker. You will speak of the spirit of these men for many years to come, God willing. A grand day."

Old Irish had lost no enthusiasm, and settled into a chorus with just enough rhythm to aid the innate faculty that prodded men to put one foot in front of the other, shuffle, hobble, and hop. Proudly.

@@@

Redbeard and his crew of marauders now numbered six in all, including Dogtooth. The cadence of that loud singing soldier would mask their movement, for now, Redbeard thought. Dumb luck was the best kind.

"Hold up." The men were bedraggled, tired, hungry, and hung over. Their impatience in waiting to attack the column of crippled soldiers was exceeded only by their fatigue, and several would have preferred to simply lie down in clover and sleep for eternity.

But hunger moved them. Fear of being arrested, tried, and hanged moved them. Each would kill for a single ration of hardtack. Kill each other, if necessary. Only their nagging fear of Redbeard kept them from stealing from each other or quitting altogether.

"We'll take 'em at the next break for rest. They are due a noon meal, so's keep an eye out for large portions for cooking. It's tough to tell in this brush, but someone must have cooking gear. You two," he pointed at Rufus and Farr. "Wait for them to pass, then come up the right side. When I fire, and I'll fire first, attack the end of the last platoon."

"Where will you be when you fire?" This from the gaunt boy, a pathetic man-child who demanded more in attention and explanation than he could ever contribute in practicality. This one avoided Dogtooth during the day, and was clearly frightened of him at night. Wretched and pitiable.

"Between the first and second platoon, near the front. I will shoot the colonel on his horse. That's when we attack, not before. But be quick. Some of the cripples can still move and shoot, so do your damage, take what you can, and then run back the ways we came."

Dogtooth sucked an imaginary cuspid. "Meet at the still? That's far."

"No. There's a shanty we passed an hour ago. Meet there first. If you're not there in an hour after the job, you're on your own."

They all silently agreed.

"You two don't attack at first. Once we hit 'em, stay on the ground and provide cover for us to escape to the rear before you hit the last platoon. Your powder dry?" Redbeard expected these worthless animals to be too confident, easily discovered and cut down by the crippled soldiers. Rufus and Farr nodded in assent. He needed these four to create a diversion for his own escape.

"You two," Redbeard was talking quickly now, trying to confuse the foul brothers, "hit the middle of the line, but start shooting right away. Cause panic. Break the column, steal what you can, and break through the other side, then run to the shack." These two couldn't find their own arses with a map, he thought. They'll get cut down, too.

The bandits were all smiling and nodding, impressed with the feigned leadership. Redbeard would have these idiots shooting each other if he could time it right. The goal was not food, or weapons, or anything else of value. The mission was to assassinate Time.

Redbeard's cousin was hanged by Time two years before for stealing from the union dead on the fields of Antietam. Dragged, beaten, roped and hanged within minutes, with two others. Redbeard had been there and was stripping corpses with them, but had escaped being caught through his own cowardice. He was silent as to the coming cavalry and pretended to be among the dead. No use in both of us being dead, cousin, he thought then. I'll make it up to you.

That opportunity was today.

The marauders could still hear that obscene singing soldier, but they were behind the columns. With as much stealth as they could manage, they moved into position for their raid. Attack the 18th.

@@@

Sergeant Kuriger had begun to stare at the back of Colonel Time's head, willing him to glance back. Time was talking to the boy, who was chatting back over his shoulder, and Kuriger was certain the colonel couldn't hear a word the child was saying. Henry Two would laugh, Time would laugh, and Old Irish's cadence was still strong, though much abbreviated from the ramblings of an hour before. Irish had also drifted to the rear of the march, winded and struggling to maintain his rowdy humor.

"Oh Sally Oh Sally we's marching my dear,
The 18th is coming the rebels will fear,
We slide and we shuffle,
We hobble and hop,

Tell Richmond we're coming and right up their rear!"

Several men responded with each chorus, but fatigue was setting in, as well as anticipation. Officers normally don't brief soldiers on tactics and a potential drill without trying it out, and each man and boy knew a morning drill was imminent.

Colonel Time could feel Kuriger's eyes on his neck. He turned his head toward him to confirm it, nodded, and started to raise his arm.

Lieutenant Anderson, at the head of the trailing third platoon, had spent most of his time on the march encouraging his men to keep up with the platoon ahead of theirs without running, without panic. Gaps would come and go, bunches would come and go. All due to terrain, with a balance for alignment met very quickly. His unit maintained. Marching with injured men broken by war could be more trying than an actual pitched battle.

His wind was good, although when he tried to bark encouragement it came out squeaky, and his men struggled not to laugh openly. Anderson knew they still called him Teacup when he was out of earshot, and sometimes well within it. No longer Teacup out of derision, he knew, as they liked him, but real respect is hard-earned. These soldiers of the 18ᵗʰ were rough men who held their leaders to sometimes impossibly high standards. Some standards were minimal: aloofness, ferocity if necessary, but usually just stoicism. Teacup still required more time to develop the latter.

A crash and a snort to Anderson's left in the woods, maybe twenty or thirty yards. The brush was less dense here. There was a ridge over fifty yards away, barren of pine trees to his immediate left, rising steadily to a forty foot elevation from his head. Steep enough to avoid. Not for deer, though. But why would an animal be moving along with us with all this singing? *No.*

Anderson realized that marauders were about, and willed his voice to command, as their lives might depend on it. He would not fail again.

"ALARM! ALARM! Bandits at our left flank! Assume fighting positions! RIGHT NOW."

@@@

Time had begun to lift his arm to signal a break when he heard an officer raise an alarm. Could that bellow have been Anderson? He wondered. Perhaps the young lieutenant was taking initiative with a drill. Good for him. He turned his horse to see the double column formation fall to the earth and face outbound, crawling to the side of the road looking for rocks, dirt, logs or cover of any kind.

Time dismounted, handing the reins to Henry, who automatically wiggled into the saddle, much too short for the stirrups. Time took two steps, saw the frozen part of the line at Anderson's position over fifty yards behind, and knew this was no drill.

The single shot took him on the right side of his chest, and exited from his hip on the opposite side with a gaping hole of bone, blood, and gore. Time held his ground even in death, and slowly fell, stiff and lifeless, pitching forward with a gracefulness that belied the brutality.

Kuriger knew instinctively that Time was dead, and he looked out to the direction he presumed the shot came from. He could see a large figure moving quickly up the slope of the ridge, toward the rear of the formation, fighting through brush and between trees.

Anderson saw the assassin, too, and his command was clear and strong. "Maintain your position, do not break your line, take no shot unless point blank. Steady." And then he launched himself into the woods, up the tree line in pursuit of the running figure.

Trenton reared back and nearly threw young Henry, who gripped the reins and hair and held on, crushing his knees into the horse's neck. Instinctively he pulled back, wheeling the horse around. Trenton stomped with both front legs, reared again, wheeled again, and began a fast trot and then a full gallop down the road ahead of the 18ᵗʰ, toward Port Royal. Henry Parker clung to its reins and neck, his legs waving like pennants in the wind.

Anderson saw the marauder they called Redbeard, with a second man at his heels, sprinting uphill through the sparse brush amongst the pines to the ridgeline above. His impulse gave chase, Anderson in awe of his own audacity. With one eye on the second marauder and watching his own foot strikes, he kept an angle on Redbeard. He thought of his sidearm but lacked any confidence in using it. Running with a pistol is futile, would only give him less leverage on the run with his stump arm, and when he would have to fire, if he had to fire, the single round would be needed for close, final work. Anderson knew that Redbeard had killed someone, and from the intensity of the commotion he heard behind him from the front of the column it would have to be either the colonel, Kuriger, or God forbid Henry Two. One of them was probably dead, he thought. The coward Redbeard was notorious for cruelty and mindless savagery.

I will run him to ground, Anderson thought, capture or kill. The 18ᵗʰ would have its vengeance. He heard several rapid shots from the formation but no cries of pain. Then a loud volley, followed by intermittent shots probably from panic.

Dogtooth trailed Redbeard and fell, grabbing his ankle, howling in pain. Redbeard slowed from fatigue and carrying his rifle, gasping for air, with a wide-eyed grin of triumph mixed with fear. Less than twenty yards from him was Anderson, still in a full uphill sprint, and he would catch him at the crest of the ridgeline. Anderson wondered why Redbeard never looked his way. Redbeard turned back in disgust at Dogtooth, and slowly turned to face beyond the ridgeline. He was spent. A dark black boiling cloud on the horizon was moving quickly toward them.

He spied Anderson too late, his heavy breathing and bravado making him too confident. Anderson, five yards away, drew and leveled his pistol, angled upward, hand shaking slightly, footing sound, prepared to shoot.

"Drop it."

Redbeard hesitated.

"Surrender or I shoot you here. Now," Anderson's voice breaking ever so slightly.

@@@

The trail platoon, prone except two, took two rounds in rapid succession to its position. None hit anything but trees on the opposite side. The lone standing soldier was Thunder, carrying Cal on his back. Rufus and Farr started to charge the formation as instructed, but faced the giant bluecoat before they could breach the left column. The plan foiled, their escape confused, the two ran awkwardly parallel to the road, turning and running, stopping and falling.

"Shoot the bastards," from Lieutenant Swanson. "We're not taking prisoners. We canna afford to feed 'em."

Five rifles roared from the column. All five soldiers would later claim to have made a kill shot, at about thirty yards, and an intrepid corporal with one leg swore for years his single shot killed both. The two marauders went down hard, and did not move again.

Old Irish was up and pointing. "Who's that on the ridge?"

Cal yanked Thunder to face where Irish was pointing.

"It's Redbeard, and Teacup has a pistol on him."

@@@

The foul-smelling pair of marauders had breached the center platoon and killed one of the 18th, a one-armed soldier from Pennsylvania who could not bring his bayoneted rifle up fast enough. Fatigue, hunger and sweat are terrible conditions when surprised, and the consequences here were fatal. A call for the doctor was made, forgetting or not knowing he was not there. Stinnet called cease fire, struggling to stay calm. The dishonor of shooting a crippled man, not armed for a fight, will haunt these animals, the Lieutenant thought. I didn't get a good look at them.

There was no loot, no food, nothing of value. The two quickly withdrew the way they came. A few seconds to shoot one bluecoat, and then it was over. If the two simpletons had crashed through both columns, they may have run into Rufus and Farr, and they might, just might, have killed each other, as Redbeard had designed.

@@@

Redbeard glared at Anderson. Still breathing heavily, he yawned, infuriating the lieutenant, who stammered, "Oh, you're tired now? Drop it."

Redbeard looked evenly at Anderson, placidly, paternally, but still gasping for breath.

"You may be in command now, lieutenant. Your colonel is very dead."

"Drop it."

"No, I think not. You'll not shoot." A deep sucking breath and exhale.

The quickening black clouds swirled like a cauldron over their heads, the air now thick and humid. On the far side of the ridge, down a steep slope to Redbeard's rear, was a pond not quite overflowing, but with some movement to it. Big enough for a canoe or two to make long turns, for geese or ducks or for children to swim to their heart's content. Looks deep, Redbeard thought, that's not the way out. I cannot swim.

Lieutenant Anderson fired. The round burst from the pistol seemingly slow enough to see, grazing the left shoulder of Redbeard, who threw his head back and turned slightly, exclaiming in mock surprise, "AHA". He raised his rifle flatly to Anderson, staring malevolently. Anderson had fallen to his knees.

"I won't miss from here, lad. I knew you couldn't kill me. You'll now wish you had." He pulled the trigger.

@@@

"Jesus help us, the lieutenant fired and fell and that animal Redbeard is pointing his rifle at him!" Cal nearly screamed in frustration.

Old Irish spat, locking his rifle into his shoulder. "I have him. I can hit him from here."

"No unnecessary firing. . ."

The rifle coughed, barely kicking, Irish holding his shot true.

@@@

The horse moved swiftly, effortlessly, eager to run, flying to stay ahead of the impending downpour behind it, the boy clinging to its neck.

"Be good, Trenton, be good," was all Henry Two could say above the rush of the wind and heavy air before the rain, and for many long minutes he kept his eyes closed, moving his frame in rhythm as an extension of the horse's head in each stride.

@@@

The officers rode two abreast, six total, less than two miles away from the Port Royal command post, at a gentle canter. The exercise of the horses was the reason and excuse for the break from the flurry and monotony of routine. The day was warming, and dark clouds threatened to the north, far enough that a mile or so respite of easy conversation would be an indulgence few would argue against.

Doctor Gordon Bernhardt, colonel, was sandwiched ahead and behind by burly junior officers on steeds of real strength. He had borrowed a nag from the officer's stable, as his own horse was being shoed. The nag had a light step, was energetic, and seemed capable of a burst of unprovoked power, or if by whim. It had its scars, both from spurs and switch, but must have sensed that the doctor was a temperate sort, and walked with a spring.

Bernhardt was smiling broadly, and confided to Captain Morris on his left.

"I am looking forward to seeing the company of the irregulars, captain. I know the general has much faith in their commander. The march should be safe, I suspect."

"Yes, doctor. The general has great respect for Colonel Time. . . and for those men. He and the colonel go back many years." Morris looked skyward to his front, north. "They'll have it easier if there's no rain."

Over his shoulder, Major Owens, an artillerist of true skill, half-barked.

"It'll rain, gentlemen. And soon. But it is too pleasant to turn back right now." He extended his arm briefly and quickly over his head, and all stopped.

"I hear. . . perhaps our ponchos are in order, if it's rain, but. . ."

From the north, the rumble of horse's hooves peppered the hard earth of the road to Port Royal.

"Quiet," from Morris.

In half a whisper, Owens said, "Sounds like only one, Morris, but hell-bent on getting somewhere. Captain, draw a bead on the rider and prepare to fire if this goes awry."

Trenton's full gallop, with the boy at its neck, would seem not to be prepared to halt. Owens dismounted, as did two others, all thinking silently that it was a stray with a yoke of some kind on it, racing to get ahead of the impending storm. As Trenton rode closer it slowed, reared, pivoted once, faced north, and then pivoted again, facing the stunned officers.

"There's a child on it," said the doctor, who began to struggle to maintain control of his own nag.

"Sirs! Sirs! We're being attacked!"

"Who, boy?"

"The 18ᵗʰ!" And with the proclamation made, Trenton reared, turned, keeping the child balanced, and darted back down the trail from where it came.

"Dear God," whispered Bernhardt, and his nag took off, quick on the heels of Trenton, perfectly aching to run on the flat stretch of road ahead.

Owens commanded, "Captain Morris, back to post. Bring well-armed reinforcements at the double quick. The rest of you, we ride as hard as we can."

The four officers took off in hasty pursuit as the blackening sky grew and rolled, pregnant with rain.

They overtook the doctor on the nag in short order, but not until after the skies opened up. The four horsemen continued ahead without any restraint, the rain not diminishing the wet dust and mud thrown by Trenton ahead of them on the rapidly murky road. Claps of thunder or rifle fire? Impossible to discern at full gallop, the officers rode their horses harder, rain pouring from the darkening sky, a cauldron from the netherworld, driving to rescue the 18th.

The sky descended black as pitch.

The road swiftly became a quagmire, and the horses fought against their riders, slipping, turning, stopping and stepping forward and into each other. Visibility was worse than poor, and the officers, duty bound, shouldered into the downpour, and they cursed and prayed they would not be too late.

@@@

Redbeard's rifle did not fire. He heaved, "Damn wet powder." His running and reloading had been hopelessly bungled.

Anderson realized death was not to come on this ridge at this vermin's hands. He sprang to his feet, charging, but within a yard of tackling Redbeard, a bullet punched the marauder's shoulder and the two men thumped into each other.

The rain descended and crashed to the earth.

As the men folded over each other, sliding and tumbling down the reverse slope of the ridge toward the pond, neither had a sufficient grip on the other. The momentum of the downhill fall was sped up by a torrent of mud, and both collapsed and splashed awkwardly into the edge of the pond that churned with the cascading rain. The sky and air were black.

Caked in mud, scrambling for purchase of his feet, Anderson grabbed the coat collar of Redbeard and pulled him close.

"You die today."

Redbeard howled in pain, mud and water being sucked and spat, roaring an oath to kill the boy lieutenant. Bone shattered on his right side, Redbeard fought to get his cudgel loose, to grip and strike and free himself from this one armed child in a man's uniform.

"You crazy bastard, I'll kill you yet. Now's your time to run," Redbeard bellowed.

The two foul marauders and Dogtooth came at a sliding trot, one entering the water too quickly, falling in, nearly being entombed in mud as the rain came harder.

Anderson and Redbeard were up to mid-thigh at the pond's edge. Anderson saw one route, and that was the center of the swirling mass of water. Each step took him deeper, pulling the howling man by his coat, and the urgency of Redbeard's fear grew hysterically, the pond now at their waist and rising, boiling in the static warmth of the storm.

"I can't swim you prick," cried Redbeard, grasping at what he believed was his weapon, his right hand not working, still enraged, eyes pleading with Dogtooth and the others to do something.

Anderson stepped again, then again, an iron grip on Redbeard's collar with his one hand. The three marauders on the pond's edge stood, reached uselessly, mouths agape, dancing foot to foot, unable to commit to a rescue of their leader, unsure of how deep the pond was, or how deep the young lieutenant's conviction would be.

Anderson took three more steps, now thirty feet from the pond's edge, and stepped into a hole. Redbeard raised his cudgel, screamed in agony, and plunged it where the boy officer had submerged. The water churned as the two men fought beneath the peppered surface. Then only Anderson's head broke the choppy plane, and his gasp for air became a clear hoarse shout.

"Tell father!"

He plunged back under the roiling water.
Neither rose again.

@@@

Thunder had already been moving at double-time up the ridge, right after Old Irish made his shot, Cal urging him to charge harder. Cal called out at the apex of the ridgeline before the reverse slope, "Down and slide on your rump," and Thunder did, cradling Cal. They spun once, twice, and Cal seized a prickly bush, slowing but not stopping the fall. Feeling the tug from Cal, Thunder dug his heels hard into the mud, and they stopped before reaching the pond, several yards from the three now incredulous bandits.

Cal had seen the Lieutenant and Redbeard go down.

The two foul ones took a last glance at the swirling pond, shook their heads in unison, and waddled and ran south, toward the road, and without a word they were gone.

The rain stopped.

Dogtooth was frightened. He could follow the others, or try to go up the ridge where now several soldiers stood and knelt, one rifle awkwardly trained. His back to the pond, his recourse was to go through the giant, or the small one with no legs.

Thunder rose and stood his ground, but began whipping his head back and forth, vainly trying to hear Cal. Anything. Nothing. The only sound his own harsh breathing through his nose.

"Cal."

"Yes."

"Where is the lieutenant?"

"Gone. Stand tall."

"Shut up both of you." Soaked and wild-eyed, in two quick steps Dogtooth grabbed Cal by his hair. Cal writhed in pain, defiant and silent, fighting but afraid that if he called out he would scream. He was determined not to show fear to this animal or his fellow soldiers. Dogtooth chuckled.

"I'll have fun with you, boy." He pulled his knife. "If any of you," he called out, "Come near, I'll cut his throat." He pointed the blade at Cal's chin.

"Cal."

"Yes."

"Stop fighting him."

Cal stopped, keeping his hands close to his head. Dogtooth's grip hardened, the knife's tip absently cutting the soldier's chin.

"We'll be walking out of here now," rasped Dogtooth. "Be a good boy."

"You ass. I'm not walking anywhere." Cal grabbed the knife wielding hand with both of his, twisting it away, pulling with all his weight down, down and away. Dogtooth was shocked at the power in the small one's hands, the calluses and vise grip.

Thunder took a slogging step toward the sound, then another as Cal strained against the larger man's strength and fear, and Thunder could feel the heat in the battle for the knife, could feel the exertion of an uneven fight to the death, and inched closer.

"Let go let go let go" was all Thunder needed, a steady stream of panic from the maw of the bandit, and he had his hands around Dogtooth's head and squeezed, pushing down. The three fell to their knees.

"Hurry, George, I canna hold on."

Thunder drove the marauder's head into muck and mud in half a breath, suffocating Dogtooth in the brackish earth. Cal let go, and George felt the weight of the final fight of the man slump and twitch, placing his knee on Dogtooth's chest, and then sank the head backward, engulfing the wreckage of his face and head in sludge and grease at the pond's edge. In moments it was over.

"George."

"Yes."

"It's done."

@@@

"Halt! Who goes there?" The rifleman at the point saw the shadow of a horse many yards out, and although the rain had slowed substantially, his challenge was deadened before it reached its ears.

"That's a friendly, private. Not many marauders have horses hereabouts," Kuriger said calmly. Loudly, he said, "Everyone hold steady, keep your position. I will see what is what."

Kuriger quick-stepped toward the now walking horse, recognizing Trenton and the boy clinging to its neck. He sighed, swallowed, and bit his cheek, thinking that the boy was dead, the horse gone, while his honored colonel and friend was growing cold and stiff surrounded by frightened cripples. He managed a smile. God is good, he thought. He has returned the child and the horse.

Kuriger quickened his pace to the approaching horse as the rain abated, steady but soft, unrelenting in its fuel for mud and impassability.

"Henry Parker. Two."

"Yessir?"

"Thank you for coming back. You worried me."

"I brought help, sergeant-sir."

The boy was exhausted, and Kuriger saw his mouth was bleeding, and his hands were cut from his own nails. Trenton snorted and whinnied as Kuriger took the reins.

"Well, I'll be damned. God is good, Henry Parker!" Kuriger then saw four horsemen, union, officers all, trying to gallop, moving steadily, purposefully, without concern for safety. It occurred to Kuriger that these men came at speed, not knowing if a fight was on, an ambush, or a rout. Their sense of rescue exceeded their fear of danger. To be expected of officers, thought Kuriger, if not always demonstrated, they being a cautious group by training.

Owens spoke to Kuriger.

"Is the situation secure?"

"Likely, sir. Sergeant Kuriger, command sergeant of the 18ᵗʰ. One known casualty by sniper fire. The platoon commanders, four lieutenants, are determining a casualty count now. Mobility once the rain started was . . . difficult, sir."

"Have someone take these horses, sergeant. We will walk the inside of your perimeter. Dismount."

"Sir, I will precede you. The men know me, and they might be skittish."

"Of course, Sergeant Kuriger, of course. Lead the way."

The rain stopped. The air was cooling. A light breeze picked up, and the scent of pine was carried down the road as if on a carriage.

Kuriger nodded for two privates who came without hesitation, and they took the reins of the four horses, each of them with a one-handed grip, pinching their respective weapon under the other stump arm. The horses would need the strong hand, and the soldiers could always drop the reins and quickly grasp the rifle and prepare to bayonet. Their powder was now useless. Henry Two stayed on Trenton, now sitting in the saddle. One of the privates tried to nuzzle Trenton affectionately, the other nodded to Henry, and Trenton strained to take his own lead behind the group with Kuriger.

The sergeant called Lieutenant Swanson to the head of the formation. He now stood at the shoulder of Colonel Time, in death's repose with one hand on his chest, his campaign hat covering his face.

"Colonel Time is dead, sir. He never knew what hit him, I believe."

The rescuing officers, now joined by Rhoads, stared down at the fallen commander.

"Damn it all. Lieutenant, are you in charge here?" asked Owens.

Swanson hesitated, but spoke directly without emotion. "No, sir. Lieutenant Anderson is in command, sir. He saved us. He heard the ambush coming, sounded the alarm, and we hit the ground just as we had drilled. We felt the bullets fly over us, sir. Lieutenant Anderson saved the company."

He couldn't save his colonel, Owens thought.

"Stay here, lieutenant. A much larger contingent will be here shortly. And a doctor will be here as well. No accidents, understood?" Owens could not help but stare at the lieutenant, a broken man in body and spirit, struggling to keep his wits and provide leadership, his only responsibility. The lieutenant's massive effort to stand tall could not now compensate for a lost ability. A shame. He knew Kuriger would see to unit cohesion and discipline from here on.

"Lead the way, sergeant."

Kuriger stayed a few paces ahead of the officers, not quite protocol, but certainly realistic given the unknown tactical situation.

The soldiers were kneeling in puddles, straddling pools, or looking for dry ground and an unseen enemy. Their attention focused on the officers walking inside the columns, Kuriger at the lead asking questions. Sharp glances into the wood on each side, but it was clear the danger had passed. Whoever had attacked them came away with nothing, and had taken away lives for nothing. Soldiers get light headed after a fight, and the drenched road, mud-caked uniforms, and sodden boots and weapons made for a curious and pathetic sight. They grinned through it, and a few started to laugh at the absurdity of it all. Owens and the officers asked each man, in turn, if they were able.

"Any casualties?"

"Have you seen any marauders? Enemy?"

"Can you stand?"

"Are we secure?"

"Any dry powder?"

Single word answers for the most part. A chatty thick necked soldier missing an arm spoke rapidly of the two marauders who broke the center of the line, but they ran away, empty handed, except for killing the conscript who stayed on, from Pennsylvania he thought, name of Mattey. As good a man as ever wore the uniform.

The last platoon had the worst of it, and the most to report on. There were several gaps in the line. The soldiers with both arms had remained in position, their leg injuries making the climb up the ridge all but impossible.

"We killed two of 'em, sir. Right there in the road. We left 'em there. They're good and dead."

Old Irish spoke up.

"Kuriger, there's hell to pay up that ridge. Teacup ran up there, and I know I shot Redbeard. They fell over the other side, and I don't know what the hell is over there. That giant fool Huntred and that sack of grain on his back took off up there as soon as I got 'im. Three or four others took off after them."

Owens asked intently, "Point true for me."

Old Irish pointed, and the officers took off up the hill.

Kuriger asked him, "That major is looking for an excuse to murder now, Irish, any other shooting?"

"No. But I'd run up there and murder, too, if I could."

"Look. . . go to the head of the formation, James. Go now." And Kuriger started up the slope in trail of Owens and his officers, stopping halfway, turning and looking in private torment as Old Irish moved steadily to the head of the column.

@@@

Old Irish hobbled up to Roberts, who stood sentry at the fallen form of Colonel Jon Time. Roberts glared as the older soldier knelt at Time's side, but said nothing. Irish slowly pulled the hat from the face of the commanding officer of the 18th.

"Oh, Jon."

Time's visage was anguished, as if in death he still felt pain. Eyes closed, mouth open and off-center, chin slack. There was little blood, as both near instant death and the rain had proved bloodless as to the mortality of Time.

Irish tried to move the colonel's jaw in place. "That's better, Jon. You would approve, I think."

Roberts looked at Irish in a new light. "Jon?"

"He was my younger brother," Irish said in answer, as he looked at the colonel's face for several long minutes.

Kuriger approached, having been told by Owens to stay with the formation. He placed his hand on Old Irish's back.

"I am sorry, James. He was my only friend."

"And you were his, Kuriger. He believed in your destiny together. I just didn't think he would die without you and me, too."

James Time closed his eyes, bowed his head, and saw Jon and him as boys shouting and running in a way only uninhibited brothers can laugh about, games without form, recalling and forgetting in the hazy mist of memory. He thought of summer hours of snap-the-whip and how he and Jon would always hang on, their hands secure on each other's wrists, impenetrable, fused, never to be broken. As boys they would look at the setting sun on the Delaware and boast of the future. James prayed, for an end to death, for a dry shoe, for that legless kid Cal Straw, and Kuriger and Perks and all of them, but most of all he prayed to keep the boyhood image of Jon Time.

@@@

Cal's eyes were glazed, his voice just above a whisper, "I saw the whole thing, George. Lieutenant Teacup drowned himself to kill that Redbeard." He looked out at the now calm pond. Two bodies floated and bobbed, both face down.

Thunder reached out to Cal, and gripped an arm and a shoulder, pulling away from the body of Dogtooth. Cal was sitting, unmoved, staring at the inky pond. The sky began to lighten, the clouds faded to grey, a streak of blue poked through. Steam from Cal's bare head lifted and swirled.

"You're cut, Cal. I can feel it. Your arm. Oh, Jesus."

"I'm okay, it's from that brush when we fell, I think, maybe the knife."

"Help! Hey, get down here, help us. He's bleeding. We need HELP NOW."

The soldiers chattered on the ridge, deciding whether to leave their position, and one man tried to amble down, but slipped and fell every two steps. He became wedged, now helpless himself. This was not a slope for soldiers without all their faculties, so they hollered instead.

A bald private cried out, "Thunder we cannot make it down there, we'll break a neck. Maybe I can do it. Both my legs are good. Hold on! Hold on! Pressure!"

The bald private turned and scrambled down from his position. The fallen soldier was stuck on a rock, and he began a slow, low wail, injured. A third soldier, who held a rifle ready to fire, had one leg working wrong and had lost the cane he used to correct it. "I cannot go up or down, Thunder."

Thunder heard their despair, knew they were giving it their best. It would have to be enough. It would never be enough.

The bald private had both legs, but his hips were of worse use than the end of his left arm, which came to a point above where his elbow should have been. He faced the hill, one step downward, two oblique, two down, one oblique. He abandoned his pack. Pulling his knife, he reared back and drove it overhead, hard, into the earth at his hip. It held. He shimmied his knees, pulled with his right arm, body now tight to the mud. When the hilt touched his chest, he dug his knees and feet and stump for purchase, raised his knife from the earth, leapt down and drove it again, deep, and started his descent anew.

It would take an hour to go forty feet at this pace, without sliding in an uncontrolled fall right at Thunder and Cal, making the attempt at rescue akin to an assault. The futility of the effort made him curse and stop the progress, slowly resting the crown of his head on the muddy slope in resignation.

Thunder knew it would take more resources than those he could hear. "Cal."

"Yes."

"Cal, I think the bleeding stopped. But I can't tell from the wet and mud."

"Yeah, I dunno, but I'm feeling very bad." Cal looked at the pond, and leaned back into the mud. "The lieutenant and

Redbeard are floating in the pond, George. Teacup drowned himself to kill Redbeard. He said something, shouted something, before he went under . . ."

"'Tell father.' He yelled, 'Tell father.'" A thick emphatic retort from George.

"Yes, yes. Tell father. Do that, George, for all of us. Tell," and Cal closed his eyes, his head rolled back, and the rattle of his death came from him softly, hoarsely, finally.

George understood, and did not want to understand. He was amazed and frightened and wild with anger.

The howl of Thunder met Owens at the top of the ridge.

@@@

A company of union soldiers arrived within the hour, assessed the situation, and requested all hands prepare to move out post-haste.

It proved time consuming to rescue the giant, and to retrieve the remains of Lieutenant Anderson and Private Straw. The bodies of Redbeard and Dogtooth were buried shallow and unmarked. There was some debate if all four union soldiers should be buried with honors at the hill crest, to include Colonel Time and Private Mattey. James Time requested that his brother be returned to Port Royal, and Major Owens firmly assented.

It was decided for the time being to memorialize the site, and Anderson and Straw's remains were buried with due solemnity on the ridge facing the road to Port Royal.

"We'll return with proper markers."

@@@

17

Port Royal

★

*U*pon the arrival at Port Royal, there was much chaos and talk of disbandment of the 18th, specifically the Second Battalion, over the next two days. It came to a head inside General Grant's personal tent.

Captain Hendricks found himself fighting a losing turf battle, and knew that Grant would soon hear the wrath of the medical corps' officers. Colonel Bernhardt, the ranking doctor of Grant's forward movement, was especially incensed, and most persistent. An audience was granted.

The general was abrupt. "Yes, colonel, what is it that is so urgent?"

"General," Bernhardt paused dramatically, "the Second Battalion of the 18th Veterans' Reserve Corps is decimated."

"Stop it, colonel. Their commander was a good friend of mine. Assassinated. A crippled young officer from Ohio showed much personal bravery, sacrificing his own life, I am told, and who killed, by hand, a marauder of notorious reputation. Another legless soldier died in a struggle to the death of a known pederast. This is a setback, but the unit has spirit and drive. . ."

"GENERAL GRANT."

Grant was cut off by the astounding gravity of the colonel's outburst.

"General, over a hundred sixty men started that march, and arrived a day late by the Grace of God and less than fifty could stand muster today or are now even remotely fit for light duty. Their injuries are worse, spirit notwithstanding, my surgery is overwhelmed, and the long-term casualties from the march are in the dozens. Men who will need more rest, even more limb removal."

Bernhardt paused to catch his breath and his emotions, and failed.

"These men are more than fatigued. They are almost broken beyond repair. I INSIST this be stopped now. I INSIST these men, every last one, be hospitalized in a permanent facility if needed or separated from active service at once. I INSIST."

Grant glared at the shaking colonel. Hendricks looked down at the toes of his own boots.

"You are dismissed, colonel."

"General. . ."

"Enough. I will take this under advisement."

The medical officer departed quickly, and Grant walked toward the entrance of his tent, and stared out. He then placed his head in his hands. He believed the command tent too busy, and this private tent was his only refuge. It had become much smaller today.

Grant wanted to do right by his men, his soldiers all, who wanted to serve. But the grand idea was now wrong, and he could not be distracted by sentimentality.

"General, we can start scaling this back," said Hendricks thickly. Grant was appreciative he was there.

"Ask General Rawlins to come by. Right away."

@@@

Kuriger had kept himself a discreet distance from Grant's tent. The doctor's strident outburst had resonated too loudly, and most of the officers and attendants had vacated the area. As Doctor Bernhardt erupted from the tent, Kuriger saw the man walking angrily and stooped, burdened but whole. Then Hendricks followed in a hurry.

Grant emerged.

Kuriger saw Grant from the distance, and was returned with a direct stare. Grant smiled. Kuriger began to turn away, but the general rose to his full stature and smartly saluted Kuriger, him alone. They held each others' presentment, and Kuriger saluted briefly and self-consciously. Grant's hand fell, and he pivoted smoothly back into his tent.

"Well, I'll be."

Later that morning, after having a too brief and too friendly audience with Rawlins, Grant's right hand general staff officer, Kuriger knew that his destiny would be limited to supervision of guards for the duration of the war, if he was fortunate. Still, he had unfinished business with several troops, and set about to this responsibility.

After writing to Lieutenant Anderson's father, a chore he refused to ask for assistance on, he sought James Time, without success. Kuriger never saw him again. Some of the 18ᵗʰ simply left camp, without pay, unconcerned with consequences. Kuriger assumed the older Time was one of those few.

The Port Royal encampment was a flux of incoming and outgoing units and materiel, and the next day would be momentous as Grant left for Petersburg and to secure an end to this madness. An end that Grant and Kuriger and any union soldier worth his salt knew could only come with the annihilation of the Confederate Army under Lee. The war, and the death around its purpose, was wrong in its inexorable pace of years. Yet it was right to seek its end, even though the agony of more death and the separation of common civility and good judgment were required. It had to end, for good and forever.

Kuriger walked purposefully through the hospital ward of a converted church. The giant George Huntred was apparently asleep, legs jutting out from the end of the bed, arms wide and unsupported. The sergeant approached with a quick step and George cocked his head to the rush of air and sound.

"Who goes there?"

"Sergeant Kuriger, Huntred. Are you injured?"

"No. I just don't want to get up, is all."

A plump, pretty girl was at the giant's side.

"He drinks little, eats less, and I don't think he sleeps."

"I don't want anything. I don't want help."

She hissed, "But you're not hurt. There are men outside laying in the dirt."

George thrust his chin skyward, defiantly.

"Laying in the dirt? There is less honor in being alive, Missy. I am glad I am, but I do not know why Cal died and I live. I have to make my life mean more than just being. And I can*not* if I can*not* see."

Kuriger interrupted the argument.

"What's your name, young lady?"

"Sheila." She smiled.

George stirred. "I'm getting up. I want to go outside and lay in the dirt."

@@@

Kuriger had little concern for Henry Two. He knew the child was readily adopted by the medical corps, as Doctor Bernhardt had taken the boy under his wing, and that he would be looked after. Although Henry was relegated to cleaning and sharpening knives and polishing boots and running small errands, he was engaged, he was included, and he appeared happy. Kuriger could never know that Henry Two was shaken to his soul and consumed by a distrust that would never be too far from the surface. Henry Two had seen evil and would forever fight a hatred in his heart. Henry's perceived exclusion from full acceptance, as an outlier and a slave child, would prevent his love and trust from ever embracing those he saw as his keepers.

Kuriger knew his own life of service would end as certainly as this awful war. He would not return to Central New York and had never had a home beyond an army barracks for nearly twenty years. He knew no other life. His pain was acute. His calling was interrupted. Kuriger did not know what he would do as the years went by, but he knew now he would serve in this army as long as it kept him.

Kuriger's faith in a higher power was his only solace. To do less than his duty was inconceivable.

@@@

Corporal Perks, now assigned to the medical corps, kept an eye on Henry Two.

"Tomorrow you begin to learn letters and ciphering."

Henry was curious, but did not see what was so special. He witnessed that most men were anguished when they held paper in their hands, and only found peace when gazing at the sky, or the stars, or a roaring fire. Learning letters would not bring back his parents or his baby sister.

Sensing Henry's confusion, Perks told him, "You'll be glad to learn reading, Henry."

And he did. Henry Two would trust this soldier Perks now, and would take each man on his own merit in the future. Henry Two would let his instinct guide him, judging a man by his actions, not his words.

@@@

Sheila took George out into the summer sunshine. George stayed stoop-shouldered and tentative in his steps, allowing only Sheila's hand on his elbow. The girl chattered away, sensing the giant's unresponsiveness was warming to feminine sounds. Sometimes he blushed, and she was rewarded with a smile when she asked about his closest friend.

George began speaking of Cal, animatedly, and they both stopped walking near a small copse of white birch. He told her that he had carried Cal Straw on his shoulders, and that he was legless and small and bony and how they needed each other, and had saved each other.

"His name was Cal? A blond boy? My cousin was with him when he lost his legs last year. She loved him so. Delaney was younger than me, and the winter took her away."

She stifled a sob, eyes blurry from the memory of Delaney's laughter, her own envy of the girl's spirit vanishing with her cousin's death last winter, and Sheila had decided to imitate the sheer life spirit of her sweet young cousin.

They stood in quiet, George now silently consoling the nurse. Awkward minutes passed.

"I can carry you if you're tired, missy, on my shoulders."

"Call me Sheila. I suppose that would be fine."

She placed her hands on his forearms and yelped as he easily and gently gripped her waist and slid her across his high back, her middle cupping the back of his head, her ample chest brushing his right ear.

"Oh, my," she said.

"Oh, my, yes," he said.

He told her how Cal would direct him. She tried to be his eyes, and they stumbled and laughed and quickly developed a tenderness with each other. One hand of hers kept her skirt pressed to her legs, his left hand free, her left hooked his head, her right on his chest, his right on her back, her scent overwhelming him and her senses acute.

"What's wrong?"

"I should let you down."

"I don't want to get down. I like being here."

"Miss Sheila, you don't understand. It is painful to walk.'

She whispered to him, he set her down, she turned him with her charms, and they strode behind some shrubbery and although George could not see her, he could imagine her fully.

@@@

18

Grief's Miracles

★

*T*om Anderson was bereft.

The summer heat hastened and bleached the air, the trees, and the earth under his feet. The roads through Ohio and Pennsylvania and the hills through Maryland and Virginia were covered in the same gauze of grey trapping the brightness of the sun and releasing the warmth of each day steadily. The arc of the sun moved in rhythm to the man, his horse, and his cart, slow and purposeful.

It had taken four weeks of travel to get from Mingo Junction, Ohio, to this singularly marked spot north of Port Royal, Virginia. The horse was too old for more than three hours' work in the morning, and maybe two in the afternoon. To coax more out of the beast, Anderson had walked instead of ridden in the cart he planned to use for his son's remains.

The sun was his friend but the bane of his travel. The rain was a blessing from heaven, but slowed his progress even more. He slept in the rain, ate in the rain, sat and stood in the rain and stared at the clouds and the stars and the wind in the trees, and the relentless puddles and running water at his feet.

It had been twenty-seven years since Tom had come home to Four Mile and left his dreams behind, and he had aged. He reflected on his life over the month of walking to Port Royal, and remained alone with his thoughts more than not. It had taken over a week for word to reach him about his son Will. He left immediately, pitifully under-prepared for the journey.

His agony was sharp, compounded by his wife's silent grief. Tom had dedicated his life to preserving a small town and raising a family, both to survive. His only son had learned and watched and gone off to this war no better equipped for its brutality and cruelty and permanence than any other schoolboy.

His guilt consumed him, and he wept silently several times a day, every day. Tom's tall tales over the years of his too-brief service without any real experience had been foundational in his son's growth, and had created an expectation of high honor in combat. Foolish.

The army was helpful throughout. A detail was assigned to exhume Lieutenant William Tecumseh Anderson's remains so his father could bring him home. First Sergeant Kuriger had volunteered to assist Mr. Anderson and had brought the three man detail, all able-bodied soldiers, to the basin where his son had died. They discussed in short unpoetic tones the propriety of taking the lieutenant's remains back to Ohio. Unsanitary, unnecessary, unrealistic. Mr. Anderson clung to one thought. Would his son be disturbed here? And there was the other soldier who lay with Will, the private who saw him last, the only witness to Will's act of courage.

Kuriger had bedded his detail down for the night. It was too late in the day to dig, and there was a drizzle. He offered to have Anderson share his tent, but was emphatically told no, thank you. The sergeant left the grieving father to his cart, worn horse, and another night alone under the stars, now mixed with a light and steady rain.

Anderson knew the task was unwise, but he could not countenance a homesteader digging a privy ten years from now and not knowing of the remains of heroes being ground under pick and shovel.

In the rain, the relentless rain, two figures stood by on the crest under a large pine, a man and a woman. The man was huge, head covered, faceless. The woman was bundled, her shape unknown, seemingly half the size of the giant. Only her fluttering hands gave notice of her youth, hard working, but young and soft nonetheless.

Anderson would sleep under the wagon. No fire tonight. He cradled his head on his forearms on the side slats of the cart. He knew the horse would not make it with the added weight of his son's remains. He was also nearly penniless, and would have to get by on the charity of others. He tried to pray, but could only conjure the fleeting image of a mourning people in song, decades before. Anderson suppressed a sob.

"Sir." A girl.

He snapped alert. The figure on the crest. He assumed a defensive posture. "Where's the man with you? I have no money. There are soldiers. . ."

The giant was only a few feet away, his hand now on the girl's shoulder. The quickening darkness and drizzling rain was making it difficult to see.

"Can we help you?" sweetly, earnestly, from the ruddy-cheeked girl.

The giant spoke. "I knew your son, the lieutenant. He saved our march from marauders."

"Ah. You must be Thunder. Good Lord, Kuriger told me of you."

"This is Sheila."

She interrupted. "His wife. His betrothed, really, we'll marry soon. But we want to help you, to bring your son home, if you'll let us."

Anderson looked at the couple, the wide-eyed stare of the girl and the giant who Kuriger called Thunder staring down at the girl, no, staring. . . at nothing. He then recalled Kuriger telling him the soldier was blind, a member of the 18ᵗʰ and possibly the strongest man in Grant's Army.

"I have no money to offer you. I barely have enough food."

"We have nowhere to go, now. We could travel with you," said the giant.

"I don't think I can return to Ohio with my boy. The horse is faithful, but not up for this. I couldn't sell or trade her now." He choked back an involuntary sob.

"I can pull the wagon, sir. Sheila can guide me. We won't be a burden, and I have some pay that will get us to wherever you go."

"Where's Ohio?" asked Sheila, curious.

Anderson smiled for the first time in a month. It pained him.

"Thunder, what's your name?'

"George. George Huntred. Family was from Pennsylvania, north of Philadelphia. But I am not going back."

"We're looking to start new where we can just be," Sheila smiled.

"George." Anderson was struggling to stay composed.

"I was there, sir. I heard him clear as day. Cal saw what the lieutenant had to do to kill the man called Redbeard. As evil a man never lived. I am here to tell you your son killed a killer, a coward who murdered our colonel and a runaway slave family and untold other terrible things. Tea. . . Lieutenant Anderson. . . saved many of us we know and will never know. That scum Redbeard needed killing. And I heard your son tell me; tell. . . *me*, to tell *you*, he done it. He did, and he died doing it. I will not rest until I have paid my respects, sir." Thunder's blank gaze never left where Anderson stood.

Anderson was moved. He had heard of his son's apparent sacrifice from Kuriger, but attributed it to the graciousness of army leadership to a mourning father.

"Thank you. I am grateful for your witness."

"Mr. Anderson? We, well, George, has a request."

"What is it, child? Anything in my power. . ."

George said thickly, "My friend Cal Straw. He saw your son drown that scum Redbeard. Cal died in my arms by the edge of the pond. I couldn't save him. Could, could we take him to Ohio, too? They are buried together. I would not want to separate. . ."

"Oh. Oh. Let's try to sleep on all this. I am thinking, well, let me rest on all this."

Sheila said softly, sweetly, "We have our own tent, Mr. Anderson. Would you join us? It's dry and you'll rest very well, sir. And we have army rations. Sergeant Kuriger has been most kind to us both."

And the three stayed in the tent, dry and warm. Anderson slept especially well. The youngsters fidgeted a great deal, and he feigned sleep appropriately. He wondered if they got any rest at all. Anderson remembered being young and in love and happy and not a little scared so long, long ago. And he dreamt of Brigit, and knew that first and foremost he had to ease her pain, with all possible haste.

At dawn the giant soldier was up and standing outside the tent, staring directly at the stark white rising sun. Anderson bolted quickly to a makeshift privy, and on his return the girl passed him to use the same. The soldier had not moved for many minutes.

"I can see where the light is coming from, I think, through the skin, I can see it. Not sense, but really see. I turn my head, and it dims. When I stare right at it, then the sun, the light of it, is clear. Am I facing the morning sun right now?"

"Yes, yes you are."

"What if I can see? If we cut this away, then I could see?"

Shelia had witnessed George's revelation to Anderson. She hustled herself in the direction of Kuriger's camp.

Minutes later Kuriger was in front of George, touching his face, asking questions, testing each eye in turn, first with the sun, and then with an open flame of a rag tied to the end of a stick. The left eye was dead, but George winced when his right eye was too close to the flame, and then forced himself to look right at it.

The solemn murmurs became excited bursts, everyone was shocked, and even Kuriger whooped.

"Well, damn. We need a doctor."

"Go ahead and cut, sergeant, I know you'll do it right."

Anderson barked no, no, no we'll get a doctor you've waited long enough let's not muck it up now, and everyone laughed in relief. Kuriger agreed, and he persuaded the trio to join him to Port Royal, for a proper doctor to attend to the giant's little miracle.

So the three left not for Mingo Junction, Ohio, that morning, after a prayer and tears, but to Port Royal, leaving Teacup and Cal to their rest on the hill between the pond and the road. They walked with the horse, and without the wagon.

@@@

Anderson and George and Sheila started their trek to Ohio a week after the surgery in Port Royal. Colonel Bernhardt examined George and realized that the right eye was moving unopposed and rolled under the lid toward light on impulse. It was decided that the lid had fused shut during the flash fire months before, and that the finality of George's sight was presumed. Kuriger was amazed, and then silently cursed himself and every man in the U.S. Army. All had failed George Huntred. All had failed him because they were afraid to approach him, to examine his wounds properly. He had been written off as blind, crippled, and beyond repair. It was curious that the legless boy, Straw, never noticed the potential for improvement, nor had the girl who spent every waking hour with him.

Before the cutting, finished in seconds with a straight razor, Bernhardt told George it would hurt, and then was knocked back by the booming laugh, like thunder.

"Nothing will ever hurt, again, sir. Nothing."

The trio began the journey to Ohio with the sun at their backs, and the cool summer morning bracing their stride. The reflected light of the sun off the leaves of trees sparkled like thousands of pearls, glowing and winking with joy. George and Sheila were playful and exuberant, and several times ran ahead of Anderson, darting into the woods, and then would come up behind him, flush and grinning.

Ah, he thought, to be young again. He would hurry home to Brigit.

@@@

Letter to Parson Mills, Chaplain of the Veterans' Corps, Port Royal.

Reverend Mills,

I witnessed today an extraordinary connection among the aggrieved and the grieving. The remains of Lt. William Tecumseh Anderson, the man who slew Redbeard, and Private Cal Straw, both late of the 18ᵗʰ Regiment, Veterans' Reserve Corps, Second Battalion, are interred in hasty but precise graves at the crest of a hill next to a basin where the men died. A flash flood had occurred there a month ago during the march of the 18ᵗʰ to Port Royal, just before the disbandment, as I know you are well aware. The location is on the east side of the ridge before the fork to Richmond. I was part of the detail with 1st Sergeant Kuriger to remove the Lt's remains so his father could bring his son back to Ohio. It was decided to keep the remains of both men in place, with stone markers.

Private George Huntred, the blind soldier who carried young Straw on his back for a month before the march, had kept vigil at the grave after the return to Port Royal. He was given permission by the command to accept an immediate discharge. He has lived under the stars with a young girl who we all know as a nurse, the orphan Sheila. They had both been faithful to the gravesite for over a month until Mister T Anderson arrived and then Sgt Kuriger was detailed to assist Mr Anderson in any way practical.

Parson, God's Grace was on the soldier and the girl, who pledged to help Anderson in whatever he required. Thankfully he chose to keep the graves undisturbed.

I know the property fairly well. It was my brother's land. He is gone, too, having fallen to typhoid in '62. He was a rebel soldier. I have known the property has been deeded to me, but not that I want to live on it during a war, not much I can do with it. Parson, it's like Mr. Lincoln said, it is hallowed ground. I want to make that permanent. I have no inclination as to what will become of me, let alone what will happen to all that land, but if I cannot give some of it back to God Almighty I might never get to see all of it, any of it, when the war ends, or whether I will ever be allowed to settle there, being in Virginia. I am educated enough that if we do not memorialize the place, soon, then I know it will be forgotten.

This letter is my last will and testament that if I shall not survive the war, that the land be dedicated for whatever purpose the church sees fit, but that the final resting places of Lt Anderson and Pvt Straw be made plain and public and proper, and be respected for all time.

I am of sound mind and body, Reverend, and I do attest that these are my wishes.

> *Your obedient servant in God's Name,*
> *G. Harold, First Sergeant, US Army*
> *August 1864*

@@@

19

Tomorrow

*T*he high whine of traffic from I-95 mixed with the low tonal echoes in the washboard of central Virginia. Off ramps every mile or so connected the interstate to bedroom communities and other like-minded towns and hamlets. They all had traffic and congestion in common, all were in a hurry to get from here to there. One ramp off I-95 led to a four lane tributary with malls and lights and pleasant pre-fabricated happy places to eat, outside Fredericksburg on Route Three.

Travelling east, and there's one of many off ramps, and the third traffic light off one such perpendicular exit, after the strip malls, then an intersection that veers hard south, and the four lanes merge to two, and an alien traveler would think he had emerged into a new world of ranch homes, lush green lawns, large pines and oaks and white birches, all mature and full in the early summer morning.

One short but time-consuming mile into the neighborhood and the waffle terrain curves to make routine traffic deliberately slower, and then abruptly stops. A new center of commerce, a new four lane road, traffic lighter, and a blue and yellow sign "Welcome to Four Corners," faded and forlorn, speaking from a once proud and recent but soon forgotten past.

Through the light, normally a one cycle wait on a Saturday, and past the blue roof of a busy IHOP, another light, past a short strip mall, and a children's park opens up on the left. Everyone in Four Corners knew where "Teacup Fields" was, with two baseball diamonds unfenced, a cross country dirt track, a macadam walking path through a wooded grove, volleyball and a couple little tyke playgrounds with jungle bars and slides. At 10 a.m. on any Saturday it was busy. During Little League season it was a joyfully chaotic riot of children yelling and parents laughing and scolding, the sounds of balls and bats and encouragement and the occasional crying complaint.

Teddy was poised to run into the fray.

"Let's check it out first, Teddy. Get our bearing." Burt was mildly winded, flush and feeling pretty good. He was surprised Clarence joined them for the walk, and even more impressed how fast Clarence walked the half-mile to the Fields.

"Can we go watch the game, Grumpy? Dad says I can play next year. Did you play baseball, Clarence?" Teddy pronounced Clarence's name a little different each time he spoke, which was often during the walk from breakfast, to where they now stood, overlooking the circus of normal kinetic fun in the basin below.

Clarence smiled wistfully. "Yes, Teddy, I did play ball. Pretty good, too."

"I want to play shortstop like Derek Jeter. Or centerfield. Or catcher. Or. . ."

"Teddy! Teddy! You and your grandpa can come down here!" A cute but harried Mom was corralling a couple of youngsters Teddy's size at a swing set nearby, and the shouted invite came out like a plea. Her big smile wiped the anxiety of her cry away. "Hiya, Burt!"

He laughed and waved. "Hey, Gayle! Be right down! Go ahead, Teddy, we'll catch up." Teddy ran screaming down to his friends and was welcomed with yelps and hollers as if a returning hero.

Clarence said, "This is a great place, Burt. We had one of these parks in Jersey, a little smaller, when I was a kid, but I don't recall it being so, uh, nutty." They both laughed.

"Thanks for the company, Clarence. And for your service. I have to admit that I feel a little small, 'cause I played for fun-zees, and you guys played for keeps."

Clarence smiled. "That's funny. I appreciate the thought. But the truth is that I went in, most of us did, because guys like you were watching. This was our turn. It could have been you, too." He sighed. "But I'm here now, it's all good. The Lord has walked with me, I think. And I'm grateful for today."

"Really, why?"

"I got a free breakfast out of the deal."

They both laughed knowingly, shook hands firmly, and for many long seconds just stood there.

"God Bless you, Clarence. You're a better man than me."

"Thanks. More than you know."

They released their tight grip, and Clarence looked at the shimmering trees around the field, suddenly snapping his fingers.

"Oh, hey, I have a business card. Here. I'll be staying in Four Corners with my sister for the summer until college starts in the fall. I'm gonna take another run at that."

"Why, that's great! I'll call you. This may mean a few beers at the VFW, though, sound good to you?"

"Took you long enough to ask, Burt. Heck, yeah."

They chuckled again, and shook again. Burt wouldn't let go.

"Hey Burt, this place is real pretty. What's this park called?"

"Teacup. Teacup Fields."

"'Cause of the basin here? Shaped like a cup?"

Teddy screamed as if struck by lightning. Both men flinched.

"Hell if I know. Duty calls, Clarence; into the fray I go." Burt started walking down to the playground.

"I gotta run, Burt," Clarence grinned, throwing his thumb over his shoulder. "Call me."

The End

End Notes

$\mathcal{T}$he U.S. Civil War is so heavily documented, explored, explained and treated that it is rare indeed that an original work can be cobbled together. I hope this small book is an exception. This is historical fiction, not a history. But the true facts surrounding the 18th shape and give credibility to the story here.

The 18th Veterans' Reserve Corps, formerly the Invalid Corps, was active throughout the Civil War in varying strengths. The general movements of an element of the 18th during the spring and summer of 1864, from the outskirts of Washington, and to Belle Plain by boat, guarding prisoners, and culminating in the two day march to Port Royal, are factual and a matter of record. The change in designation from "Invalid" to "Veterans" occurred also, as did the mission and general composition of the First and Second Battalions. The initial robin's egg blue uniforms and the change back to standard issue may seem a silly affectation, but it was an important decision during the conflict. In my preparatory reading, I found that the respect afforded the injured or crippled soldier was of paramount concern, second only to Grant's need for the able-bodied to stay in the field engaging the enemy. The uniform truly does more than identify: it dignifies.

The characters and plot are fiction and my invention, with one obvious exception, with whom I took great license to give invented dialogue and mannerisms.

The idea to put a story to the true history of the 18th was influenced by Bruce Catton's iconic and award-winning work, <u>A Stillness at Appomattox,</u> which remains arguably the finest concise history of any period of our country's worst war. The story of the 18th needs to be told often.

Our nation can be held accountable for its regard for the injured who risked all to defend her. The wreckage of a soldier's sacrifice will expose the soul of his country. The respect afforded the injured soldier's care can make him either humanity's refuse, forgotten, or a human monument to the nation's faith and spirit.

I pray <u>The March of the 18th</u> is worthy of every wounded soldier's sacrifice, past, present, and in the future.

@@@

Fifty percent of author royalties for this book will be donated to charities for wounded veterans.

Acknowledgements

I wrote this book for those who have served, and for those who will serve.

Jimmy Z. is a childhood friend of my family, and he deserves a special mention here. Because of him I started this book.

My brother Matt intensely reviewed the manuscript, and it is a better book because of his attention to detail. Glen R. and Jim H. were most gracious to read a near completed product, and offer their observations. To say I trust these people with the intimacy of a first published work is to speak volumes of my respect for their discretion and good judgment.

My wife Maureen and my daughter Eileen read the manuscript and lived with my daily hectoring for feedback. Angels, both.

For everyone's advice and support, and for all things large and small, thank you.

Lastly, I told Maureen I wanted to do this, and her lifelong expectations for me have made me a better man. And a very happy one.

> *"To friends and food and family,*
> *To life and love and liberty,*
> *God Bless our troops for all time, and may*
> *God Bless the United States of America."*
> Old and unattributed toast.

CPSIA information can be obtained at www.ICGtesting.com
Printed in the USA
LVOW05s1105181114

414307LV00012B/167/P